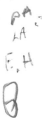

# SHANNON'S WAY

# SHANNON'S WAY

•

## Charles E. Friend

**AVALON BOOKS**
NEW YORK

PRINTED IN THE UNITED STATES OF AMERICA
ON ACID-FREE PAPER
BY HADDON CRAFTSMEN, BLOOMSBURG, PENNSYLVANIA

To my wife Rosemary,
without whose support and loving care
the writing of this story would not have been possible.

## Chapter One

Clay Shannon stood on the front porch of his home, watching the late-afternoon sun as it sank slowly toward the distant mountains.

Beyond the porch the rough ground dropped sharply down into the busy mining town of Whiskey Creek. The settlement's ramshackle collection of buildings sprawled along the slope, clinging precariously to the rocky hillside. The structures that were nestled on the lower part of the hill were already in shadow, and here and there oil lamps began to glimmer in their darkened windows. It was such a peaceful scene that Shannon could not help but think of the contrast it made with the violence that had stalked the streets of Whiskey Creek when he first rode in. Years had passed since then, six years in fact. To Shannon it seemed like centuries.

He watched as the lengthening shadows crawled up the ridge toward him, stealing the light. *Sundown*, he thought. *The end of another day. And the days pass so quickly now.*

1

*Soon it will be sundown for me, too, I suppose. Time is catching up with me.*

Across the valley, the sun was disappearing below the horizon. Its last rays struck the surface of the little river that flowed through the valley, the river that had given the town its name. The reflection of the dying sunlight seemed to turn the surface of the water red. *Blood red,* thought Shannon. *Blood red.*

As the dusk deepened, a chill crept into the air. Shannon shivered a little. *Getting cold,* he said to himself. *Winter's coming. Or is it something else, some sort of premonition?*

A horse whinnied softly in the little corral behind the house. Shannon stepped down from the porch and walked around the building to lean on the split-rail fence of the enclosure. Just visible in the gathering darkness, the buckskin colt moved up beside Shannon and nudged his arm with its nose. Shannon rubbed the animal's neck affectionately, remembering another buckskin horse, now long dead, that he had ridden into Whiskey Creek when he first arrived to challenge the evil that was gripping the town by the throat. That, too, seemed a long time ago. In another life, almost.

With some difficulty, Shannon forced his mind back to the present.

"Well, my friend," he said to the buckskin, "I guess that's enough gloomy memories for one evening." The horse tossed its head as if in agreement.

Shannon gave the animal a final pat and started back toward the house. Lights shone from the windows, and inside he could see his wife Kathy setting the table for the evening meal. As he entered the kitchen, she looked up at him and smiled.

"Good evening, Sheriff," she said teasingly. "How many people did you arrest today?"

Shannon laughed, shaking off his somber mood. He

kissed her lightly, conscious even after all these years of the curve of her body and the gold of her hair.

"Nobody around here to arrest anymore," he said with mock regret. "Whiskey Creek's become respectable."

He unbuckled his gun belt and hung it on the peg beside the door. The lamplight gleamed on the blue steel of the old ivory-handled Colt revolver.

"Take off the badge, too," Kathy said. "It makes you look too official at dinnertime."

Shannon chuckled and unpinned the star from his shirt. He dropped it into the pocket of the shirt and settled into one of the chairs beside the table.

"Where's the offspring?" he said.

"Bobby!" Kathy called. "Come get your dinner!"

Clayton Robert Shannon, Junior, came running into the kitchen with all of the enthusiasm that might be expected of a healthy, hungry four-year-old. He hugged Shannon happily and then climbed into a chair, beaming across the table at his father. Shannon grinned back at him. *He's growing up fast*, he thought. *With his mother's hair and eyes.*

They ate dinner in a leisurely fashion, the food accompanied by the little boy's lighthearted chatter. When the meal was finished, Shannon arose from the table and walked over to the kitchen window to gaze out into the night. His wife began to clear away the dishes.

"Kathy," he said abruptly, "I'm thinking of quitting." Kathy Shannon stood very still for a moment, absorbing what he had just said. Watching her reflection in the glass, Shannon could see the troubled look on her face.

"You must do as you think best, Clay," she said. "If that's what you want, it's fine with me. But are you sure it's the right thing for you to do? For yourself, I mean. You told me once you'd never stop 'carrying the star,' as you call it, because that's all you've ever done."

Shannon nodded pensively.

"I remember," he said. "I said it one day when we were walking beside the river, before we were married. Well, it's just a thought. Can we talk about it a little more after Bobby's in bed?"

"Of course," she said. "I'll only be a moment."

She took the child's hand and led him into his bedroom. Shannon went into the living room and sank into the big leather-covered chair that faced the front windows. He knew that Kathy was right, that it would be hard for him to hand in his badge. He had been a lawman all his life, taming towns all over the frontier during the most turbulent period the American West had ever known. But that era was fading now, and Shannon was growing tired. Very tired.

*Maybe it's time*, he thought. *Maybe I'm not good enough anymore. Worse yet, maybe I'm not needed anymore. Maybe—*

The front door of the house exploded off its hinges and came crashing into the room. It bounced across the floor toward Shannon's chair, scattering splintered wood and broken glass along the carpet. Before Shannon could react, a huge, bearded man wearing a dirty linen duster charged through the door, bellowing like a crazed bull. In his hands he held a double-barreled shotgun, and by the time Shannon had leaped to his feet the twin muzzles of the shotgun were pointed squarely at his chest.

"You're dead, Shannon!" the man shouted. "I've come back for you at last, and you're cold meat now!" He raised the shotgun and curled his finger around the twin triggers. Shannon stared down the barrels of the weapon and knew that he was looking into eternity.

"Why?" he said, playing for time. His mouth was suddenly very dry.

"You know why," the gunman said.

"No, I *don't* know why," said Shannon. "What's this all about?"

"No more talk!" the man bawled. "This is it! Good-bye, lawman!"

Shannon tensed his muscles for a last desperate effort to seize the shotgun, but even as he did so he realized that he would never reach the other man in time. He braced himself for the impact of the buckshot.

A heavy glass jar came flying through the kitchen doorway and struck the bearded man squarely on the forehead. The jar shattered and the man staggered back, blood and fruit preserves dripping down his face and into his eyes. He roared an obscenity and tried to bring the shotgun back to bear on Shannon.

"Clay!"

Shannon wheeled. Kathy Shannon was standing in the doorway holding his Colt revolver. She tossed it to him across the living room. Shannon caught it, cocked the hammer in one smooth motion, and fired twice point blank into the gunman's body. The man grunted and fell backward, an expression of utter disbelief on his face. As he went down, he squeezed the triggers of the shotgun, sending twin charges of lead shot smashing into the ceiling.

Shannon sprang forward and kicked the shotgun away from the fallen man. Then, still covering the intruder with the Colt, he pulled the man's six-gun out of its holster and threw it into a corner.

The entire episode had taken less than thirty seconds.

The would-be assassin lay doubled up on the floor, his hands clasped to his stomach. Shannon knelt beside him.

"Who are you, mister?" he said. "And why do you want to kill me?"

The man glared up at him, his features contorted with pain and hate.

"You're done for, Shannon," he gasped. "They'll get you. They'll get you *good.* You'll see."

"Who?" Shannon said. "Who'll get me? Come on, man, you don't have much time."

The man struggled to speak, but could not form the words. His eyes were becoming glazed. He coughed, took one more breath, and died.

Shannon stood up. Kathy was beside him now, looking down at the corpse.

"Do you know him, Clay?" she said. Her voice quavered a little as she spoke.

Shannon studied the dead face carefully, searching back through his memory for a clue as to the man's identity. Then it came to him.

"Leach," he said. "His name is Leach. He was one of that bunch of thugs that ran Whiskey Creek when I first came here. He and some other gunmen pulled out and went north when we cleaned up the town. Said they were headed for Montana."

"But why would he come all the way back here to kill you now?"

"I don't know," Shannon said. "I suppose he must have carried a grudge against me all these years because I broke up his gang and killed his friends."

He put his arm protectively around Kathy's waist, and they stood there together for a long moment. The full horror of the evening's events was just beginning to dawn upon them, and Shannon could feel Kathy's body starting to tremble against his arm as the inevitable reaction set in.

"Say, lady," he said hoarsely, forcing a smile, "you did all right just now. Where did you learn to heave a jar like that?"

Without answering, she turned toward him and buried her face against his shoulder. Quietly, she began to cry.

Shannon held her close against him, wanting to comfort her but not knowing how.

"It's all right, Kathy," he whispered. "It's all right now."

Their son appeared in the doorway, clutching a stuffed toy bear and staring wide-eyed at his parents and at the bloody devastation around them. Wiping away her tears, Kathy went to the boy and took him in her arms.

"I'll put him back to bed," she said, carrying him hurriedly from the room.

As Shannon bent down to search the body, the faint sound of a horse's hooves reached his ear. He raised his head and looked keenly out into the darkness that lay beyond the empty front doorframe. A rider was coming up the narrow path that led along the slope to the house. Shannon dropped to one knee and cocked his six-gun, watching the doorway, ready to fire. Footsteps sounded on the porch and then Shannon's one and only deputy, a not-too-bright young man named Billy Joe Carson, peered cautiously into the room. A look of wonder spread over his face as he took in the scene before him.

"Jumpin' Jehoshaphat," he said. "I was in the office when I heard the shots. Thought they might have come from your place. What happened?"

Shannon carefully uncocked the Colt and shoved it into his belt.

"Uninvited guests," he said.

"Who is he?" Carson gulped, peering incredulously down at the dead man on the carpet.

"A ghost from the past," Shannon said. "Literally."

"You kill him?" Carson asked, awed by the sight.

"No," said Shannon grimly. "Mrs. Shannon did it with a jar of preserved peaches. I just helped."

"But what was he doing here?"

"Never mind that now," Shannon said. "There may be

more of them out there. Did you see anyone as you were riding up?"

"No, not a soul," said the deputy. "There's a worn-out horse tied to a tree a little ways down the hill, though."

"Probably his," Shannon said. "Now do me a favor—go find the undertaker and tell him to come and get this mad dog's carcass off my floor."

Carson took one last look at the stiffening corpse, then vanished back out through the door and into the night.

Shannon eased himself slowly back into the leather chair. As he did so, he realized with disgust that his hands were shaking. Filled with self-contempt at his own weakness, he fought to bring his body and his emotions under control. Like most men of his profession, he did not like to admit— even to himself—that he could ever be afraid.

## Chapter Two

The first gray light of dawn was just touching the streets of Whiskey Creek when Shannon opened the door of his office and entered. Billy Joe Carson came yawning out of the back portion of the building where he had been sleeping on one of the cots in the jail.

"That you, Sheriff?" he said, still only half-awake.

"Yes, Billy Joe. Got any coffee back there?"

"Sure," said Billy Joe, scratching vigorously at his long underwear. "Last night's. I left it on the stove." He disappeared into the jail and came back with a steaming cup.

"Thanks," Shannon said. "Now get your pants on and go wake up Mayor Ford. Ask him to come down here as soon as he can. Then go to Arnold Davis's house and ask him to do the same. Bring them in their nightshirts if you have to, but get them here."

The deputy grinned and went back into the jail. He emerged again still struggling into his clothes, and departed

9

through the front door on his errand. Shannon took a sip of the coffee and winced. Too strong and too sour, as usual. Among other things the deputy did not do well, Billy Joe made terrible coffee.

Shannon opened the shutters on the office windows to let in the morning sunlight. Still carrying the cup of foul coffee, he sat down at his desk. The desktop was piled with papers, but he pushed them aside and leaned back in his chair to think. Fatigue lay heavily upon him, for he had spent a sleepless night, sitting in the darkened living room of his home with a rifle across his knees, listening for any sound that might betray the approach of further trouble. As he had sat there in the darkness, he had tried to analyze the events of the evening and what they might signify. Who were "they"? What were "they" going to do? And when? Despite his night-long vigil, he was no closer to the answers.

He was still contemplating the problem when the door opened and Elijah Ford, owner of the general store and Whiskey Creek's longtime mayor, walked in. He was followed closely by Arnold Davis, president of the Bank of Whiskey Creek. Both men were unshaven and their clothes were in disarray, indicating the rapidity with which they had responded to Shannon's summons. Shannon waved them toward the office's two dilapidated chairs.

"We heard about what happened at your place last night," Ford said. "What do you make of it?"

"Not sure," said Shannon. "Maybe just one angry gunslinger out for revenge. If so, it's over, and there's nothing else to be done. But there could be more to it than that. The man indicated there might be others involved."

"You don't think he was acting on his own?" said Davis, trying to blink the sleep out of his eyes.

"Perhaps he was," Shannon said, "but I can't just make

that assumption. When you carry a star, you can't afford to assume anything."

"If there really is going to be trouble, what do you think it will be?" asked Ford.

"That's a tough question," Shannon replied. "If Leach had friends, and something is being planned, there's no way to know what it might be, or when it might happen, or where. We'll have to take an educated guess. I'll say this, though—I don't think Leach or these other men, whoever they are, came back here after six years just because they don't like me. Obviously that's involved, but I think it must be incidental to something else, some larger plan. Anyway, I'll do what I can to prepare for it, whatever it is."

"How can we help you?" Ford said.

"No need for anyone else to get mixed up in this," Shannon said. "When it happens, *if* it happens, my deputy and I will handle it. I just wanted you and Arnold to know the situation."

Ford leaned forward in his chair.

"Clay," he said, "when you came to this town it was a lawless, violent, dangerous place. You changed all that. Because of what you did, today Whiskey Creek is a growing, prosperous community. We've got a school, a bank, a telegraph office, even a church. People can walk the streets safely, raise their kids, live a good life. We owe you, and we want to help you now."

"Yes," said Arnold Davis, the banker. "You admit you don't know what may happen. What if it's something too big for you and Billy Joe to handle alone? Let us give you a hand."

"Thank you," said Shannon. "Both of you. I appreciate your offer. But it's hard to prepare for the unknown. If there's something in the wind, we don't have a clue as to what it might be. Until we do, I'll just have to wait and watch."

"Then we'll help you watch," Ford said. "We'll swear in extra deputies. Post 'em along the street and on the roof-tops. Right here outside your office, if you like."

Shannon shook his head.

"I don't want any of the people of this town getting hurt," he said. "I'm the law in Whiskey Creek. This is my job, and my problem. If we put well-meaning amateurs out there with guns, someone will get killed. I don't want that. I'm sure you don't either."

"We can't just leave you to face this alone," Ford insisted.

"I'd rather have it that way, Elijah," Shannon said. "Please tell the townspeople that if they see anything suspicious to report it to me, but otherwise they should just stay out of it. We may be up against some rough people here, and I don't want anybody getting shot unnecessarily. All right?"

"I guess so," said Ford, "but I'm not happy about leaving you out on a limb like this. Anyway, I'll pass the word around town for you."

"Try not to scare people," Shannon said. "This may all be just a false alarm."

"Or it may not," said Ford. "Be careful, Clay."

"Always," Shannon said with a smile.

Ford got up and left the office. Davis started to follow him.

"Arnold," said Shannon, "it seems to me that if some sort of gang has plans for Whiskey Creek, the bank is an obvious target. Have you got any unusually large amounts of money in your vault right now?"

"Well, yes," Davis said. "Quarterly payroll for the mines—biggest payroll we've ever had."

"Do a lot of people know how big it is?"

"There's been some talk," Davis said. "Always is when we're holding large sums like that. Oh, I see what you

mean. . . ." Although the office was chilly, he began to perspire as the import of Shannon's question sank in. "I suppose I'd better put some extra guards in the bank, just in case," he said, mopping his brow with a handkerchief.

"I'd rather you didn't," Shannon replied. "If you fill up the place with a lot of armed and extremely nervous citizens, and there *is* a robbery attempt, somebody's sure to panic and begin shooting prematurely. The last thing I want is for somebody to start gunplay at the wrong time."

"Well, whatever you say," Davis said. "It's your neck. But if you change your mind, let us know, will you?"

"I will," said Shannon. "Thanks again for the offer."

Davis hesitated, then shrugged and started for the door. With deliberate casualness, Shannon picked up his coffee cup and gave the banker one final reassuring wave. He did not want the people of his town to worry. To his mind, worrying was his responsibility, not theirs. There was no way for him to know that by refusing the townsmen's offers of assistance, he had just made the biggest mistake of his life.

When Davis had left, Shannon got up and unlocked the gun rack behind his desk. As he did so, Billy Joe Carson came back into the office.

"What's going on, Sheriff?" he said.

"We may have a chance to earn our pay in the next day or two, Billy Joe," Shannon said, tossing him a rifle. "Get outside and watch for anything suspicious."

"Sure," said Billy Joe, going back outside. "But nothing ever happens in this town."

Calmly but rapidly, Shannon began to load the rifles and shotguns in the rack, replacing them carefully for immediate use if needed. He felt increasingly uneasy. Logic told him that there was little to fear, but instinct—the same instinct that had saved his life a hundred times in the past—

told him there was something coming, and coming soon. He could only hope that if there was to be trouble, it would come later rather than sooner, so that he would have time to prepare for it before it came.

Unfortunately, his hope was in vain. There was a sudden clatter of horses in the street, and men were shouting. In his heightened state of awareness, the noise attracted Shannon's attention immediately, because although such sounds were often heard in Whiskey Creek, usually there was little traffic on the streets at this time of the day. Shannon started toward the window to look out, but even as he moved, footsteps sounded on the boardwalk outside the office and he heard Billy Joe cry out. The deputy staggered back in through the open door; his hat was gone and there was blood running down his cheek. He collapsed on the floor, groaning. Then, out on the street, a woman screamed. Shannon's stomach turned over. The trouble, whatever it was, was happening now.

Shannon kicked his chair roughly aside and yanked a shotgun out of the rack, then raced for the office door. As he came through the doorway, someone waiting against the outside wall struck him on the head from behind. The shotgun was ripped from his grasp and he fell to the sidewalk, half-stunned. Instinctively he rolled over, reaching for his holster, but he was too late. Someone brought a boot down hard on his arm, and the Colt clattered away across the dry boards, out of reach.

Still dazed, Shannon looked up, trying to focus his eyes. A man was standing over him, and the muzzle of the revolver he was holding was trained unwaveringly on Shannon's belt buckle. The gunman was wearing a linen duster, just like Leach, the intruder Shannon had killed the previous evening. Another man, similarly dressed, stood just beside the first, covering Shannon with a rifle.

"Get up, Shannon," the first man said. "Do it slow and

keep yer hands high. One funny move and we'll blow holes in yer gut. I mean it. We'll kill ya."

"All right," said Shannon irritably, climbing to his feet. "You've made your point. What do you want?"

"Me? I just want what's in that bank up the street. But some other folks want a little more." He grinned crookedly at Shannon and then gestured with the barrel of the six-gun. "Look up there. A few friends of mine want to talk to you."

Shannon turned in the direction indicated by the gunman and saw that eight or nine riders and a dozen horses were gathered in front of the bank. The horsemen were all heavily armed, and they were watching Shannon with obvious amusement.

Shannon muttered a curse. A bank robbery, of course, the very thing he had just discussed with Davis. And for the second time in less than eighteen hours, he'd foolishly allowed someone to get the drop on him. Anger rose up in him, but he controlled himself. At the moment these men, whoever they were, held all the cards. He'd have to play his own hand carefully.

Prodded in the back by the gun held by the man behind him, Shannon walked across the street toward the bank. His heart was beating rapidly, but his mind was now clear. Even as he approached the crowd in front of the bank he was sizing up the situation, weighing the odds.

"That's far enough," said one of the riders in a harsh voice. The speaker was a tall man, perhaps forty years old, with a scraggly beard and a long, livid scar across his face. He sat astride a coal-black horse, and, like his friends, he was wearing a dirty linen duster. He leaned forward in his saddle and looked down at Shannon with cold, hard eyes. It occurred to Shannon that he had once killed a rattlesnake with eyes like that.

"You know me, Shannon?" the man said in a voice that was as cold as his gaze.

"No," said Shannon. "Should I?"

"Oh, yes, you should know me. Name's Drago. Gus Drago. They call me 'Bully.' Ring any bells?"

"I've heard of you," said Shannon evenly. In his office desk were several reward posters for one Augustus "Bully" Drago, wanted dead or alive for horse stealing, cattle rustling, bank robbery, train robbery, and at least twelve murders. One of the posters warned, rather unnecessarily, that Drago was considered extremely dangerous and should be approached with caution.

"That's good," said Drago, "because I've got a bone to pick with you, law dog. A couple of bones, in fact. Hear you gunned down my man Leach last night. You enjoy that?"

"He broke into my home and tried to kill me. What did you expect me to do, kiss him on the cheek?"

Drago laughed loudly. It was a humorless, unpleasant sound. Several of the other gang members laughed also. Their horses stirred nervously.

The two gunmen who had accompanied Shannon from the sheriff's office were still standing beside him, their weapons at the ready. Not having any other options, Shannon decided to try a bluff.

"Look, Drago," he said, "you'll never get away with anything here. Thanks to your friend Leach's stupidity in coming after me last night, I've already got a dozen special deputies sworn in and ready for trouble. Armed guards in the bank, too. Ride out now, while you can."

Drago spat into the dust.

"You're a bad liar, Shannon," he said. "Leach, blast his hide, told us all about this town, and the bank, and you. You ain't got nothin'. But that bank does—lots and lots of cash, and all of it just waitin' for us. Some of my men are in there right now collectin' it." As he spoke, a shot sounded from inside the bank, and someone cried out in pain.

"See?" said Drago. "They'll be out in a second with the pickin's, and nobody's goin' to stop 'em, least of all you."

There was another shot from inside the bank, and another cry.

"Don't hurt anybody else," said Shannon to Drago in a strained voice. "Just take the money and go."

"Oh, no, my friend. First I've got a score to settle with you."

"Why? Because I shot Leach?"

"I couldn't care less about Leach. That moron nearly ruined everything by jumping the gun and coming at you last night. Serves him right he got plugged. No, Shannon, I've come to see you about another matter."

"Which is?"

"You remember a man named Sullivan?"

"Maybe," said Shannon, thinking back. One of the men he had shot while cleaning up Whiskey Creek six years previously was named Sullivan. He had been one of the hired hoodlums sent to kill Shannon. And Leach had been part of that same gang. The pieces of the puzzle were falling into place. "What of it?" Shannon said.

"You killed him, too."

"What's that to you?"

"His real name wasn't Sullivan," Drago rasped. "It was Drago, Zeke Drago. He was my brother."

Shannon was silent for a moment, digesting this information. Now he understood what was happening. This was not just a bank robbery. Drago wanted revenge.

"Drago, listen to me," said Shannon. "Your brother was one of several men who were hired to ride in here and murder me. They ambushed me in my office, killed my jailer, and wounded a couple of other people. I did what I had to do."

"Yeah," Drago hissed, "and now I'm goin' to do what I have to do. Ah, here come the boys now."

Two men rode out of the cross street next to the bank. It was the street that led up to the top of the hill, toward Shannon's home. Shannon suddenly felt sick. One of the men was holding Bobby Shannon on the saddle in front of them.

The two horsemen reined up in front of the bank, close beside Drago and the rest. Shannon saw that the rider holding Bobby had a rope looped around the boy's neck. Bobby's eyes were wide with fear.

"You see, we just paid a friendly visit to your house," said Drago. "We thought we'd invite your kid to take a little ride with us."

Shaken by this development, Shannon groped for words. As he was trying to find his voice, four men came hurrying out of the bank with bulging saddlebags slung over their shoulders. They threw the heavy bags onto their waiting horses and mounted up.

"Ready, boss," one of them said to Drago.

"Wait a minute, Drago," Shannon said. "Let the boy go. Your quarrel is with me, not him." Then a new and chilling thought occurred to him. "Where's my wife?" he said, trying to keep his voice steady. "What have you done to her?"

"Aw, we just roughed her up a little bit," replied one of the riders. "She didn't want to part with the kid, but we persuaded her." He snickered. "Don't worry, we didn't hurt her much. Last I saw of her she was tryin' to follow us down here on foot. Reckon she'll be along in a minute."

Even as he spoke, Kathy Shannon came stumbling down the hill and around the corner of the bank. Her hair was tousled and her dress was covered with dirt. She was gasping for breath, and her eyes were wild.

"You filth!" she cried. "Give me back my son!"

"Grab her," Drago said. Two men dismounted and grasped Kathy's arms, twisting them behind her as she fought to break free.

"Let them go, Drago!" Shannon shouted. "Kill me if you want to, but let them go!"

"Oh, I'm goin' to kill you, Shannon," he said. "You can count on it. But that ain't enough. You took my brother; now I'm takin' your kid. Seems fair, don't it?" He glanced at Kathy, who was still trying to wrench herself free from her captors. Drago laughed again, then reached across to pull Bobby off the other outlaw's saddle. He lifted the child through the air and dropped him roughly onto the shoulders of his own horse in front of the saddle horn. Bobby squealed in pain and then began to cry.

"Don't do it, Drago," Shannon said desperately. "Leave him here."

"Yeah, I'll leave him," Drago growled. "After I've blown your brains out I'll leave him down by the creek for your wife. I'll leave him hangin' from a tree."

Kathy Shannon uttered an anguished cry and wrenched herself away from the men who were holding her. She ran toward Drago's horse and reached up to snatch the boy out of the bandit's grip. Drago pushed her away, grinning evilly. Kathy staggered forward again, clawing at Drago's face.

"Why, you witch!" Drago snarled. He backhanded her across the mouth, knocking her sprawling in the dust.

"Shoot her, Benny," he said.

The rider next to Drago pulled his revolver, cocked it, and aimed it at Kathy Shannon as she lay dazed at his horse's feet.

Shannon went a little mad, then. Nothing mattered to him any longer except saving his wife and son. He whirled and drove his elbow into the ribs of the bandit who had been standing to his left. As the gunman staggered back, Shannon tore the six-gun out of his hand and swiveled back toward Drago and the other horsemen. He shot the man who was aiming at Kathy, knocking him off his horse. Then Shannon swung the revolver toward Drago, hoping to bring the outlaw down before he himself was killed. Drago pinned Bobby against his body with his left arm and drew his revolver. He pointed it at Shannon, thumbing back the hammer to fire.

Then a rifle shot sounded from further up the street, and the gunman standing to Shannon's right gasped and went down, clutching at his leg. The other outlaws turned in surprise, looking for the source of the gunshot. Shannon looked too, and saw that a dozen citizens of Whiskey Creek were running down the hill toward the bank. They were armed with a variety of weapons and led by Elijah Ford. Mayor Ford was brandishing a shotgun and yelling for the others to follow him. Ford's men all began to fire at the outlaws; most of the shots went wild, but one of the bandits crumpled and another's horse bolted, creased by one of the slugs. Then the Whiskey Creek men were falling too, as the outlaws began shooting back at them. Mayor Ford sprawled on his face and lay there, unmoving.

Many men were shouting now, and horses were rearing in panic. Shannon saw that from his present position he could not risk firing at Drago because of the danger to Bobby. He started to move to one side to get a clear shot, but someone behind him smashed a rifle butt between his shoulder blades, driving him to the ground. Still holding Bobby before him, Drago got off two quick shots at Shannon, but the bandit's shying horse ruined his aim, and the bullets merely kicked up dust next to Shannon's head.

Shannon's deputy, Billy Joe Carson, came stumbling out of the sheriff's office holding his rifle and trying to wipe the blood out of his eyes. A slug took him high in the chest, and he collapsed onto the boardwalk.

Shannon saw Billy Joe fall, but there was no time to think of the deputy now. He scrambled to his feet and tried again to bring down Drago without hitting Bobby, but one of the panicked horses got between Shannon and Drago, blocking Shannon's line of fire. The rider pointed his pistol at Shannon, and Shannon shot him through the head.

The fusillade from the oncoming citizenry was getting more accurate. The outlaws were now on the verge of panic, milling about and shooting back wildly. Drago fired again at Shannon, but again he missed as his black stallion flinched under him. Furious, he flashed a glance of burning hatred at Shannon, then cursed and shouted, "It's a trap, men! Let's ride! Every man for himself!" The gang members needed no further urging; they spurred their horses savagely and began to race at breakneck speed down the hill toward the creek.

Drago was having trouble managing his nervous horse because he had his rein hand around Bobby and his revolver in the other. Shannon made one more attempt to shoot Drago, but the cylinder of the six-gun was empty. He dropped the weapon and lunged at Drago's horse, reaching for the reins. The gunman jerked the animal's head away, gave Shannon one last glare of malicious triumph, and kicked his horse into motion. He plunged away at a full gallop after his men, still holding Shannon's shrieking son on the saddle before him.

Kathy Shannon stumbled to her feet and started to run after Drago.

"Kathy!" Shannon called. "Don't—"

Drago looked back and saw the frantic woman pursuing him. Grinning malevolently over his shoulder at her, he lifted Bobby bodily from the saddle, swung the screaming boy high above his head like a rag doll, and then slammed him down viciously onto the hard ground of the street. The child's small body rolled several yards, and then lay still.

Kathy flung herself down the hill toward the place where Bobby lay and went to her knees beside him, cradling him in her arms. Shannon stooped and caught up a rifle that had fallen from someone's saddle. He took aim at Drago's distant back and fired, but his hands were unsteady and the shot missed. Shannon attempted to lever another cartridge into the chamber of the rifle, but the weapon jammed. He hurled it aside and stood there, fist clenched, staring down the hill. As he watched helplessly, Drago and his men passed from view, leaving only Kathy in the street, clutching her son's body. Even at that distance, Shannon could see that she was weeping.

# Chapter Three

They carried Bobby into Shannon's office and placed him on the bunk. The boy was unconscious, his pulse weak, his breathing erratic. Kathy hovered over him, caressing his hair and calling his name. Shannon took one agonized look at his son and then hurried back into the street to get help. Both of the town's doctors were in front of the bank, ministering to the wounded. Shannon went over to Dr. McCallum, who was kneeling beside one of the injured townsmen. Reed McCallum was a good physician, relatively new to Whiskey Creek. He was also a teetotaler, unlike the town's older doctor, Doc Purcell, who had not read a medical book in twenty years and was seldom sober after 10:00 in the morning.

"I need help, Reed," Shannon said to McCallum. "Bobby's hurt. We took him to my office."

McCallum looked up, concern on his face.

"How bad is he?" he said.

"Bad enough, Doc. Unconscious, blood coming from his nose and ears."

McCallum grimaced.

"Take him to my place," he said. "I'll be right with you."

Shannon ran back into his office, picked up his child, and carried him the short distance to McCallum's home. The doctor's office was in a small building adjoining the house. At the rear of the office there was a bedroom which McCallum kept for the use of his patients, since Whiskey Creek had no hospital. Shannon carried Bobby into the bedroom and gently placed him on the bed. Kathy knelt beside the boy, wiping his forehead with a handkerchief that was already wet with her own tears.

Shannon hastened back outside to the town's main street. Dr. McCallum was still bent over the wounded man, trying to staunch his profuse bleeding. As McCallum worked, he glanced around him. "This place is like a slaughterhouse," he said.

Shannon followed his gaze. There were seven people lying in the street. Some were groaning or calling for help, but others were ominously silent. A wounded horse was limping away from the front of the bank, whinnying in pain. Another lay dead close by. It was a terrible scene, but now only one thing mattered to Shannon—his son.

"Bobby's in your office," Shannon said. "Kathy's with him."

"Good," said McCallum. "I'll come as soon as I can."

"I need you now, Doc," Shannon said. "Not soon. *Now*."

McCallum put his ear to his patient's chest and sighed.

"Yes, I can come now," he said. "This man's dead anyway. I guess Purcell can handle the rest." He picked up his bag and nodded to Shannon. "Right," he said. "You coming with me?"

Shannon looked around at the carnage in the street. He wanted to go with McCallum, back to his son's bedside, but people were milling about aimlessly, waving guns, yelling at one another, uncertain what to do. A firm hand was needed to prevent total chaos. Once more, Shannon's old nemesis, duty, held him tightly in its grasp.

"You go on ahead, Doc," he said, nearly choking on the words. "I'll be there as soon as I can."

McCallum patted his arm. "I understand," he said. "Don't worry, I'll do everything I can for the boy." He hurried away toward his office.

Shannon stepped up on the wooden sidewalk and bent over the inert form of Billy Joe Carson. The deputy was dead. There was a look of pained surprise on his stiffening features.

Shannon retrieved his six-gun from its resting place on the boards, then hurried back up the hill toward the bank. A number of armed citizens had gathered in front of the bank, and some of them were now mounting horses, shoving rifles into their saddle scabbards and preparing to ride after the outlaws. Shannon walked over to them and threw up his hand.

"Hold it, boys," he said. "I don't want anybody going off half-cocked here."

"But Sheriff," cried one of the mounted men, "we need to get a posse after those sidewinders."

"No," said Shannon. "You people will just get yourselves killed if you go dashing off like this. Besides, look up there." He gestured at the darkening sky. "A storm's coming, and the bandits' tracks will be washed out before you get a mile. You won't even know where to look. Let me handle it."

"If we don't get started right now, they'll get away!" said another man.

"They won't get away," Shannon replied calmly. "That I promise you. But an angry mob riding blindly after them isn't the answer. Those men are hardened criminals.

They've been chased before, and they'll know you're coming long before you ever catch a glimpse of them. Even if you can follow their hoofprints in the rain, they'll leave false sign, double back, and ambush you when you least expect it."

"You ain't gonna go after them?" someone shouted. It was a miner named Bo Dapp, a chronic troublemaker who fancied himself fast with a gun.

"I'll go after them, Bo," Shannon said. "And I'll get them, too. But I'll do it at the right time and in my own way. If all you people go blundering off into the countryside like a pack of baying hounds, you'll just make things worse than they already are. Now climb down off of those horses and let me do my job."

"Not a chance, Sheriff," Dapp shouted. "We're gonna get those owlhoots, and we're gonna do it right now. Come on, men!" He wheeled his horse and spurred off down the hill. The other citizens looked at Shannon in indecision. Some of them reluctantly dismounted and led their animals away, but five of them, ignoring Shannon's plea, whipped up their horses and raced off after their fellow townsman, leaving Shannon standing in their dust.

*I should go after those idiots right now*, he thought. *If they're unlucky enough to catch up with the gang, Drago and his killers will eat them alive.*

Then Shannon thought again of his son, and of Kathy. Duty was one thing, but now it was time to put his family first. Erasing all other thoughts from his mind, Shannon ran up the hill toward Dr. McCallum's office.

McCallum was at the bedside, examining Bobby. Kathy stood beside him, pale and distraught. Shannon put his arm around her and held her close.

"What do you think, Doc?" he said. "Will he be all right?"

"I don't know," said McCallum. "He's not coming

around. Broken arm, but that's not the main problem. He's got a head injury, a bad one. It looks like a horse might have caught him on the temple with a hoof." He stood up and looked levelly at Shannon and Kathy. "I think his skull is fractured," he said. "I can't be certain, but I'm pretty sure that's it."

"What can you do about it?" Shannon said hoarsely.

"Nothing," said McCallum. "We'll just have to keep him warm and wait. He may come out of it. He may not. I'm sorry."

"Let's get him to the hospital at the county seat," said Shannon. "They may be able to help him there."

"Maybe they could," said McCallum, "but that's fifty miles from here over rough roads. I guarantee you that Bobby would never survive the trip. Bouncing around in a buckboard with that kind of injury, he wouldn't last five miles, much less fifty. No, all we can do is stay by him and hope. Again, I'm very sorry."

"There's nothing else to be done?" said Kathy in a broken voice.

"Well," said McCallum, "a little prayer might help."

Outside the little room, thunder pealed in the darkening sky, and the first few drops of rain began to pelt against the roof above their heads.

## Chapter Four

McCallum left, promising to return within the hour.

"I've got to check on the other wounded," he said apologetically. "A couple of them are in pretty bad shape."

"How is it out there, Clay?" asked Kathy. "Were a lot of people killed?"

Shannon eased her into the chair beside the bed.

"Two of the outlaws are dead," he said, crouching beside her. "And three of the townspeople, including Mayor Ford. Billy Joe's dead, too."

"Oh, Clay, not Billy Joe!"

"Yes," said Shannon bitterly. "And some of the wounded may die as well, since the local branch of the medical profession doesn't seem to be able to do much to help them. But what about you? Are you hurt?"

She shook her head. "I'm fine," she said. "A few bruises, nothing more. And you? Are you all right?"

"No," said Shannon, "I'm not. All of this is because of me."

"But they came here to rob the bank," Kathy said.

"Yes, they came for that," Shannon replied, "but they probably wouldn't have risked it except that Drago and Leach and maybe some of the others wanted revenge against me for what happened six years ago." He closed his eyes and ran his hand over his face. "No," he said, "it's my fault. I caused it, and worse still, I didn't prevent it. Leach's attack last night was a warning, and I knew it, but I didn't move fast enough. Now a lot of good people are dead because of me. And Bobby . . ." He gestured sorrowfully toward the bed.

"What will you do now, Clay?" Kathy asked. She had to raise her voice because of the roar of the rain on the tin roof over their heads. Another clap of thunder shook the windows.

"I have to go after them," Shannon said. "And I have to go now, because Bo Dapp and a bunch of other hotheads have gone charging off after the gang, and I must see to it that they don't get into trouble. I'll try to talk them into turning back, and then I'll go on alone. Maybe I'll be able to follow the gang's tracks despite the rain."

Kathy was looking at Bobby, the tears running down her face.

"Get them, Clay," she said. "Get them, however long it takes."

"I will," he said. "I promise you, I will."

He rose, touched her cheek lightly, then strode to the door and opened it. The rain whipped in.

"Be careful, Clay," Kathy called. "I don't want to lose you. Bobby and I need you so much."

"I'll be back," Shannon said. He went out into the storm with fury in his heart.

# Chapter Five

The rain was coming down in sheets as Shannon saddled
the buckskin, slipped his Winchester into the saddle scabbard, and rode down the hill out of Whiskey Creek. Despite
the rain, the signs of the posse's passage were plain to see.
They had headed northward toward the hills known as the
Swiftwater Breaks. Shannon moved slowly, watching the
tracks. The overenthusiastic mob of citizens that had ridden
off ahead of him had destroyed any sign of the bandits'
passing, and Shannon could only hope that Dapp and the
others knew where they were going. Seeing no indication
that Drago's killers had taken any other route, he followed
the posse's hoofmarks through the little valley beyond the
creek and began the long, steep climb into the hills.

Soon he was in the trees, and this made him uncomfortable because he could not see very far ahead along the
winding road. Apparently the members of the posse were
confident of their direction, however, for their tracks, now

slowly becoming lost in the rain-spattered mud, climbed relentlessly on up through the forest.

Once, when the rain slackened slightly for a moment, Shannon thought he heard the distant report of a rifle. He murmured an oath and pushed the buckskin faster, scanning the woods ahead for any sign of danger. His apprehension rose as a riderless horse galloped down the slope past him. Shannon pulled the Winchester out of its scabbard beneath his leg and put the buckskin into a gallop.

At the top of the hill the trail flattened out for a few hundred yards, stretching in a relatively straight line across a little grassy meadow. As he came over the rise, Shannon peered through the downpour and saw that out in the open area several horses were standing beside the trail or wandering next to it. On the ground near them were six bodies, lying motionless.

Shannon halted the buckskin just inside the trees at the edge of the meadow. Beyond the field the forest began again, thick and shadowy in the rain. It had been a perfect spot for an ambush, and the eager beavers of the Whiskey Creek posse had blundered right into it. If the outlaws were still there, waiting in the far tree line, they would have a clear shot at anyone who approached the fallen men.

Ignoring the danger, Shannon started forward, rifle at the ready, his eyes flicking first to the bodies, then to the distant trees. Had the outlaws moved on, believing they had eliminated all pursuit? Or were they still out there, waiting?

He reached the first body and dismounted. Carefully he examined each man, hoping for signs of life, but there were none. Bo Dapp and all the other members of the posse were dead, riddled with gunshot wounds. The gray sky and chill rain made their sodden corpses seem small and forlorn. It had been a very efficient ambush, and the posse had ridden unsuspectingly into it, just as Shannon had feared they would. Now six more people had paid for his stupidity. Some of them had been good men; some, like Dapp, had been not so good. But they had all been brave—reckless perhaps, but brave nonetheless. And they had been doing Shannon's job when they died.

*I should have come with them,* he told himself. *I shouldn't have waited to see about Bobby. I should have come with them and prevented this. Their blood is on my hands.*

He put his left foot into the stirrup and started to remount the buckskin. Out of the corner of his eye he saw a puff of blue smoke in the treeline a hundred yards away. He kicked free of the stirrup and threw himself down into the mud, just as a bullet snapped past and the sharp sound of a rifle reached his ear. The buckskin shied away, pulling the reins from Shannon's hand. Holding the Winchester close to his chest, Shannon rolled behind a dead log that lay nearby. Cautiously, he peered around the end of the log, and was rewarded with another puff of smoke from the trees. The slug struck the log, burying itself in the wood and sending splinters flying past Shannon's head. One of them planted itself in his cheek. He reached up and pulled the sliver out. A trickle of blood joined the rainwater coursing down his face.

Shannon looked around, weighing his situation. He was in the middle of the open ground, sheltered only by a dead log that was starting to look smaller and smaller. He had his rifle, but the horse was out of reach. It was raining hard, and despite his oilskin slicker he was soaked to the skin, covered with mud, and growing colder by the minute. It was a bad position to be in, and Shannon knew it. He called to the buckskin, but the young horse was not yet completely trained, and it merely bobbed its head cheerfully at him and began to eat the wet grass a few yards away.

Shannon pushed himself further down into the mud beside the log, fuming at his own incompetence.

*First I got these others killed,* he thought, *and now I'm about to get myself killed too. All the years I've been at this, and I still walked into a trap. Any tenderfoot could have done better. You idiot.*

Carefully he peered over the log toward the tree line, searching for some sign of his assailants.

*If the whole gang is out there waiting for me,* he thought, *I'm dead. But if they just left behind one or two, maybe I can pick them off before they get me.*

He watched the trees, ready to duck if another wisp of smoke heralded the arrival of another bullet, and ready to fire if the bushwhackers were careless enough to present him with a target. He tried to calm the rapid beating of his heart and the annoying trembling of his limbs. Was it fear or cold? Either way, he would need a steady hand if he was to survive.

The minutes dragged on, and then, as he watched, a shadowy figure came creeping up to the edge of the tree line. It was a man wearing a linen duster. Shannon rolled out from behind the log, brought the Winchester to his shoulder, and fired. The man in the trees threw up his hands and fell backward out of sight in the underbrush. Immediately, another rifle opened up on Shannon from a few paces to the left of the fallen man. Shannon rolled back behind the log, and the shots went high. *The bad news,* thought Shannon, *is that two of them are still out there. The good news is that there are only two. The rest must have ridden on.*

He moved to the other end of the log and gingerly peeked around it. There was nothing to be seen. He waited patiently, rifle cocked and ready, trying to ignore the mud and cold rainwater that were soaking his clothing and chilling his skin. After what seemed an interminable time, he detected movement in the trees. The second man was crawling along the edge of the meadow, a rifle cradled in his arms. *Probably trying to get someplace where he can have a clear shot at me. Can't let him do that.*

Shannon rose to his knees and fired, then chambered another round and fired again. Even at that distance he could hear the ugly sound of the bullets hitting flesh. The man yelled, and through the rain Shannon could see him thrashing about in the bushes. Shannon jumped from behind the log and ran across the meadow toward him. Vaulting over some deadwood that lay at the tree line, he crouched down and looked around him. The first man he had shot was spreadeagled on his back, a small hole in his forehead. The second gunman was squirming and moaning a few feet away. Shannon knelt beside him. It was the man who had brought Bobby down the hill to the bank.

"Well, tough guy," Shannon said, "no more women or four-year-old kids for you to beat up now, so let's just chat a bit. Where have all your fellow rats disappeared to?"

"Help me," the man moaned. "I'm gut-shot."

"Sorry about that," Shannon said. "Actually, I was aiming for your heart—if you have one. Now talk. Where are your friends headed?"

"I dunno," whimpered the man. "Get me to a doctor, please. It hurts. It hurts."

Shannon gazed coldly down at him.

"I asked you a question, mister," he said. "If I don't get an answer, I'll keep putting lead into you until I do."

". . . meet 'em later," the wounded man croaked.

"Somehow," said Shannon, "I don't think you're going to keep the appointment. Now *where* are you supposed to meet them?"

"Moon," whispered the man, looking up at the sky. "Moon. . . ."

Shannon glanced at the gray overcast above them.

"No moon tonight, pal," he said. "Now, one more time— where are you supposed to meet Bully Drago?" The reply was only a gurgle. Shannon bit his lip. He knew he would get nothing further out of the dying killer. He got up and went over to check the body of the other gunman; then, certain that he was past help, Shannon returned to the first man. The outlaw was still staring up at the black clouds racing along above the trees. The raindrops were falling on his eyes, but he did not blink.

Shannon contemplated his victim without sympathy. The odds were improving. *Two of these scum were killed in town*, thought Shannon, *and I got two more here. Four down, then. Only six or eight to go.*

He left the bodies where they had fallen and remounted the buckskin. He looked back at the dead members of the posse and felt a pang of regret at having to leave them there, stiffening in the rain. But he had work to do, and no time to lose. It must be midafternoon by now, and darkness would come early in the storm. He had to follow the gang while there was still some chance of catching them, before night fell and the rain washed out their hoofprints completely. At least now there would not be a posse to muddle up the traces of the outlaws' passage.

He rode on across the meadow and into the far tree line. The trail was climbing again, winding erratically as it skirted the boulders scattered among the tall pines. Shannon rode bending forward, partly so that he could see the tracks better and partly to shield himself from the driving rain. The temperature was dropping, and soon the rain began to turn to sleet.

Presently the light started to fade. The sleet was sticking to Shannon's slicker, and he was shivering in earnest now. The cold rainwater had long since penetrated his boots, and he could no longer feel his feet. His hands were also numb, and he had to force his stiffening fingers to keep a good hold on the reins. As he rode, Shannon massaged his left knee. The cold was making the old wound ache fiercely. He wished the chill would make his leg as numb as his hands and feet were.

The buckskin was shivering also. The sleet was caking up on his back and mane, and the horse was moving uneasily, silently protesting the weather and the tiring muscles that had carried it so far from home. Shannon clucked at the unhappy animal, urging him on.

At length they reached a fork in the trail. Shannon brought the buckskin to a halt and sat there in the gathering twilight, scanning the ground ahead of him in an effort to find some clue as to which direction the bandits had taken. It was useless. He couldn't even see the fugitives' hoofmarks anymore. The night and the rain had combined to defeat him. With the scent lost, he would either have to camp and wait for dawn, or go back. He cast around for some form of shelter, but there was none—just the pine forest climbing away up the steepening hills into the darkness.

He realized then for the first time that he had left Whiskey Creek in such a hurry that he had brought nothing with him to sustain a long chase. No blankets, no food, not a single match with which to light a fire. Shannon silently cursed himself for his haste in coming away without even the barest necessities. He was an old hand at this game, and should have known better. In his anxiety over his injured child and his overpowering desire to pursue the fleeing killers, he had made another mistake. He should have taken his time, he told himself. He should have provisioned himself properly and set out at his own pace, ignoring the memory of Bobby and the others, ignoring the recklessness of the posse in rushing headlong into obvious danger. Once again he had displayed a human flaw, and it had led him to this impasse. Now he would have to go back to town, regroup, and start all over again.

Slowly, reluctantly, miserably, Shannon turned the horse around and started back down the hillside toward Whiskey Creek.

It was almost midnight when Shannon rode up to the gate in front of Dr. McCallum's house. He sat there in the saddle for a moment, too stiff with wet and cold even to dismount. A light appeared in the front window of the house, and then Kathy Shannon opened the door and ran out to him, a coat thrown over her shoulders to protect her from the rain.

"Clay!" she cried. "Clay, are you all right?"

"*I* am," Shannon wheezed, "but the posse isn't. How's Bobby?"

"About the same. Get down and come in out of the rain."

"Got to take care of the buckskin first," Shannon murmured. It seemed to him that he was hearing his own voice from a great distance.

"Dr. McCallum and I will put him away," Kathy said. "Come on, get down and come inside."

He climbed slowly down from the horse. Leaning on Kathy's arm, he walked unsteadily up the porch steps and into McCallum's house.

"Doctor!" Kathy called as she peeled off Shannon's frozen slicker. "Please come out here. I need some help."

Shannon felt the doctor's strong hands guiding him into a chair and wrapping a dry blanket around his shoulders. With an effort, he explained to Kathy and McCallum what had happened, asking them to send someone into the hills to retrieve the bodies of the dead. Then exhaustion overtook him, and he fell asleep.

## Chapter Six

Shannon awoke to find himself tucked into a warm bed with a huge goose-down quilt spread over him. He peered around, but did not recognize the room in which he found himself. He threw back the covers, sat up, and swung his legs over the side of the bed. As he did so he knocked over a stool that had been sitting at the bedside. Kathy Shannon came in. She smiled at him, but her smile was wan and her face was very pale.

"Where are we?" Shannon said, trying to orient himself.

"In Dr. and Mrs. McCallum's bedroom. They slept in their living room so you could have the bed."

"How's Bobby doing?"

"No change. Dr. McCallum says he's in a coma. I sat up with him all night, and the doctor checked on us every now and then."

Shannon pulled himself erect. His clothes, dried before the fire that still burned on the hearth, were draped over a chair nearby. He struggled into them, then buckled on the

38

gun belt that was hanging from a hook on the wall. Out of habit, he eased the six-gun out of the holster and checked the cylinder.

"Don't worry about the Colt," Kathy said. "I cleaned and oiled it during the night. Your rifle, too. I needed something to do while I sat with Bobby."

Shannon nodded his thanks. Then he remembered that he also had things to do.

"What time is it?" he said, looking around for a clock.

"Past three in the afternoon," Kathy said. "You slept more than twelve hours."

"Forgive me," Shannon said. "I should have been with you, helping you with the boy."

"I thought it best to let you sleep. Mrs. McCallum helped me with Bobby. Not that there was much to do. He just lies there, so small and still. . . ." She put her hands to her face and began to cry.

"What are we going to do, Clay?" she sobbed. "How can we help him? And what if he dies?"

Shannon took her in his arms and they stood there for many minutes, holding each other close. At length Kathy pulled away and took his hand.

"Come on," she said. "I need to get back to Bobby."

Shannon followed Kathy through the door that connected Dr. McCallum's living quarters with his office, and together they went into the little bedroom behind the surgery. The boy was huddled under the coverlet, his eyes closed. His face was chalk white and his breathing was shallow and labored.

Shannon and Kathy sat by the bed for a long time, watching over their child, thinking their own thoughts. In his mind's eye, over and over like some sort of unending, hideous nightmare, Shannon kept seeing Drago hurling Bobby down onto the hard surface of the street, and the man behind Drago riding his horse right over the boy's body. It was a paint horse, a pinto, an animal so distinctively marked that

Shannon knew he would recognize it immediately if he ever saw it again—any time, anywhere, ever.

The hours passed as Shannon and Kathy kept the vigil. At length Shannon arose and faced his wife.

"I've got to get moving, Kathy," he said. "There's nothing I can do here. I promised you I'd find those men, and I *will* find them, no matter where they've gone."

"Don't go alone, Clay," Kathy said. "There are too many of them. Get help. Wire the county seat. Sheriff Hollister will send you some deputies."

"No. It would take too long."

"Then ask someone else. What about Pedro Rodriguez? He's still the marshal over in Dry Wells, isn't he? He helped you before and he'll help you again."

"I don't want to bother Pete. He's got his own problems."

"Well, then, raise another posse. There are still plenty of people in Whiskey Creek who'll ride with you."

"No," Shannon. "No more posses. Look at what happened to the last one. I don't anyone else's death on my conscience."

Kathy stamped her foot in frustration.

"Well," she cried, "you have to get *someone*. You've been a lone wolf too long, Clay. You've got to learn that you just can't do everything by yourself. Please don't be too proud to ask for help. Unbend a little, just this once, for my sake."

"It isn't just a matter of pride," Shannon said. "This is what I get paid for. Even if Bobby wasn't involved, it would still be my responsibility to track down those men."

"But why do you have to do it alone? For heaven's sake, Clay . . ."

"I'm going alone because I don't want anyone else along to complicate things. In a situation like this, one man can accomplish more than a noisy mob milling about, running every which way and falling all over themselves in the process. Sometimes going it alone is best, believe me."

Kathy shook her head angrily.

"It isn't fair that you should have to face this all by yourself," she said. "If you go after those swine alone, they'll kill you! You don't owe this town your life!"

Shannon put his arm around her and gently raised her chin until she was looking directly up at him.

"Listen to me," he said. "Listen and try to understand. When I put on this star I swore an oath, and I mean to keep that oath, no matter what. That's my way, Kathy. Right or wrong, it's my way, because it's the only way I know."

Kathy sighed and leaned her head against his chest.

"Oh, Clay," she said, "you're just as stubborn as the day I met you. And just as brave. And just as foolish."

"Well," said Shannon, "you're right about the foolish part, anyway. But I'm going."

"Then wait until morning. It'll be dark soon, and you can't track in the dark. Besides, Bobby may need you during the night. I may need you, too. Please, Clay, stay until morning."

Shannon nodded. Unfortunately, what she said was quite correct—he would never pick up the trail in the dark. And Bobby might recover consciousness at any time. Meanwhile, his wife needed his support. It was a request he simply could not refuse.

"You win," he said. "I'll stay with you tonight and start out at sunrise." He took her arm and guided her into a bedside chair. "You must be hungry," he said. "I'll rustle up something for us to eat while you keep watch."

She gave him a sad little smile.

"Thank you," she said softly.

Mrs. McCallum prepared an early supper for Shannon and Kathy, then went into Dr. McCallum's office to sit with

Bobby while they ate. Neither of them had much appetite, but they forced themselves to down a few hurried bites, anxious to return to their son. They were just finishing the meal when Arnold Davis and the other two directors of the Bank of Whiskey Creek came scurrying through the rain to knock at the door of the doctor's house. They asked to see Shannon, who found them standing nervously in the parlor dripping rainwater on Mrs. McCallum's new carpet.

"Sheriff," said Davis mournfully, "those bandits completely cleaned out the bank vault. Took the whole mine payroll, every dollar of it. Can you get the money back for us? There'll be a reward."

Shannon's did not attempt to conceal his irritation.

"Naturally I'll get the money back for you if I can," he snapped, "but first I have to find the men who took it. And let's get something straight right now—this isn't about money. It's about something much more important than that. It's about assault and robbery and murder. It's about a town terrorized and my wife terrorized and my boy Bobby lying in a bed next door in Doc McCallum's office, fighting for his life. *That's* what this is all about. So keep your reward, Arnold, or better yet give it to the families of the people who were killed. The only thing I'm interested in is tracking those men down and calling them to account for what they did. Understood?"

"Of course, Clay, of course," said Davis apologetically. "We didn't mean. . . ."

"Fine," Shannon said. "Now if you'll excuse me, gentlemen, I have to get back to my family."

Shannon sat with Kathy at Bobby's bedside through the long night. Eventually Kathy fell asleep in the chair, but Shannon remained wide awake, staring at the dancing shadows cast on the bedroom wall by the flickering oil lamp.

He was mentally tracking Drago's gang, trying to deduce their plans and their probable movements.

They certainly seemed to be bent on going north. They had been riding for several miles in that direction when they stopped to ambush the posse. And from the ambush site the tracks had continued northward until Shannon had lost them in the rain and the darkness. Could it be merely a ruse, a false scent designed to throw off pursuit? No, the fugitives had traveled too far for it to be that. Their goal was somewhere to the north, all right. Of that much he was certain.

But what was their destination? Were they headed for the high country that lay beyond the next range of hills? In that vast, mountainous wilderness a few horsemen could easily disappear. There were a hundred lonely trails up there, and a thousand places where men on the run might hide. Wyoming. Montana. The Black Hills of Dakota. Within a week the outlaws could be five hundred miles away, if they rode hard. How to find them? Where to begin the search?

*Wait a minute,* he thought. *That bushwhacker said something about the moon. I thought he was talking about the moon in the sky, but . . .*

Moving quietly so that he would not disturb Kathy, he slipped from the room and went out the front door. The rain had finally stopped, and stars glistened above him as he walked briskly toward the sheriff's office. The office was locked and dark tonight; Billy Joe would not be there. *I'll miss that dumb kid,* Shannon thought sadly. *I'll even miss his awful coffee.*

He let himself into the office and rummaged through his desk until he found what he was looking for. He spread the old map out on the desktop and set an oil lamp down on it to give him light. *Moon. There's a place called Moon, or something like Moon, up there in the mountains. I'm sure of it.* He ran his eyes across the map slowly, looking for the dimly remembered name.

"*Half* Moon!" he exclaimed aloud, putting his finger on the spot. "Half Moon City!" It was a tiny dot on the map, far to the north of Whiskey Creek. He should have remembered sooner. Not much of a city, obviously—that was a bit of over-optimism on the part of its founders—but it was there. The railroad that had given the town birth still ran through it on its way over the Rockies. Was this where Drago and his gang had planned to meet the men they had left in ambush outside Whiskey Creek? It was probably the rough sort of place where the bandits could safely stop, tend their wounded, get supplies, and even carouse a little before heading further into the desolate country beyond. And the dying gunman had gasped "Moon" before expiring. It was a long chance, but at least it was worth a try.

In the cold light of dawn, Shannon entered the stable behind the jail. He saddled the buckskin and slung a bedroll and two loaded saddlebags over the horse's back behind the saddle. He tucked his slicker under the bedroll, then hooked a canvas bag filled with food over the saddle horn. Next he donned his heavy coat, checking to be sure that the map was securely folded into one of the pockets. This time he was going to be prepared.

He walked the horse back to Dr. McCallum's office and went into the little bedroom where his child lay unconscious. Kathy was once more asleep in the chair. Throughout the night she had been awakening periodically to look at Bobby and then dozing off again. She had gotten little rest in the past two days, and Shannon didn't have the heart to wake her. He bent over her, kissed her hair, and went back out the door. Within moments he was riding out of Whiskey Creek, headed north. The wind was cold, but Shannon rode on unheeding, warmed by his own terrible rage.

## Chapter Seven

The buckskin horse stood patiently at the mouth of the pass, waiting. Shannon eased himself forward in the saddle and looked down the mountainside at Half Moon City. The town was tucked into a narrow valley flanked by towering peaks, now shrouded in the first snows of winter. The air was crystal clear and the majesty of the setting was awesome, but Shannon was not interested in scenery. For two days and nights he had ridden doggedly through the mountains, stopping only occasionally to rest and feed the horse. Once he had tried to snatch a few hours' sleep for himself, but the sleep was broken and uneasy, filled with disturbing dreams. Long before dawn he had abandoned the attempt, resaddled the horse, and pressed on.

Now, at last, his goal lay before him. But was this really the destination of his quarry? Or had he traveled all those weary miles for nothing? There was only one way to find out.

Shannon started down the grade. As he rode, he studied the layout of Half Moon City's streets and buildings, memorizing it for future reference. Railroad tracks ran like bright steel ribbons directly through the town, and far down the valley a whistle echoed mournfully as a locomotive pulling several cars came chugging resolutely up the tracks. To Shannon, still high on the ridge, the train looked like a children's toy. It paused briefly in front of the depot, then moved slowly on up the valley, heading west.

Closer up, Half Moon City looked much like any other settlement in that part of the country. The buildings were huddled together in the shadow of the mountains, as if they were intimidated by the grandeur around them. Some of the structures were two or even three stories high, but they still seemed dwarfed by the crags rising above them. The town was bigger than Shannon had anticipated, certainly larger than Whiskey Creek. Was this where the outlaws were headed? Normally men on the run would have shied away from a community as well-populated as this, unless they were very confident that they were safe. Shannon wondered idly who the law was here.

Yet whether or not he had come to the right place, he realized that he and the horse would have to rest here for a time. The trip through the mountain passes had been a very demanding one both for the buckskin and for himself, and like it or not he would have to stop for a while, get some sleep, reprovision, and then start out again. But start out for where? He needed some answers, and he hoped fervently that he would find them in Half Moon City.

His first stop was the tiny railroad depot. At one end of the station platform there was a window marked TELEGRAPH OF-FICE. On the other side of the window an elderly man was bent over a telegraph key, chewing a cud of tobacco and laboriously tapping out a message. When he had finished, he tossed a piece of paper into a battered wire basket sitting on his desk, adjusted his spectacles, and looked up.

"Mornin', sonny," he said. "Help ya?"

"Need to send a wire to Whiskey Creek," Shannon replied. Without comment, the telegrapher handed him a blank message form and a stubby pencil. Carefully, Shannon began to write out his telegram. Halfway through he paused and looked up at the old man.

"Is there a hotel in town?" Shannon said.

The telegrapher nodded.

"Three of 'em. Most of the folks who get off the train here stay at the Half Moon Hotel, just up the street. Ain't much, but it's handy."

"Thanks," Shannon said. He completed the form and pushed it back through the window.

" 'To Kathy Shannon, Whiskey Creek,' " the telegrapher read aloud. " 'How is Bobby? Reply Half Moon Hotel, Half Moon City. Clay.' That all? You get twenty-five words for the same price, you know."

"That's all," Shannon said. "How long will it take for the wire to get to Whiskey Creek?"

"Dunno. Has to go through Denver. Depends on how busy they are there. Coupla hours, maybe." He leaned over and directed a stream of tobacco juice into a brass spitoon on the floor beside him.

"How soon can you send it?" Shannon asked.

"Right now, I guess," said the telegrapher. "Nothin' else to do. No more trains until tomorrow."

"When you get the reply, could you send it up to the hotel?"

"Sure. We got a kid who delivers these things. Probably won't be until tomorrow, though. We usually close up here at six o'clock."

Shannon sighed.

"All right," he said. "Tomorrow morning, then. Thanks."

"That'll be four bits," said the telegrapher. "Cash on the nail, sonny."

Shannon paid the man, and watched him tap out the message. Then he climbed back aboard the tired buckskin and rode on up the street.

He dismounted at the livery stable and left the horse there, having given the hostler explicit instructions that the buckskin was to be well fed and cared for until he returned. Carrying his rifle and saddlebags, he walked up the front steps of the Half Moon Hotel and asked for a room. The desk clerk, a mousy little man with a pinched face, silently pushed the guest register toward him and tossed a battered pen down on the open book next to an inkwell. Shannon scratched out his signature, then casually ran his eyes up the page, searching for a name that might be familiar or suggestive. He did not expect outlaws to stay at a hotel, and certainly not to sign the register with their real names if they did, but Shannon was a careful man, and this was just one more possibility to check, one more stone that should not be left unturned. However, it appeared that no one had checked in for several days.

"Lookin' for somebody?" the clerk said acidly.

"Maybe," said Shannon. "Anybody new been through here recently?"

"Just you," replied the clerk. His manner suggested that he did not wish to pursue the subject further.

"There a good place to eat hereabouts?" Shannon asked.

"Café down the street," replied the man, handing him a room key. "Number twelve. Second floor, end of the hall." He watched silently as Shannon carried his gear up the stairs.

The room was small and none too clean, but Shannon was not in a mood to be critical. He dumped his saddlebags and rifle on the bed and then went out in search of the café the desk clerk had mentioned.

The place was small and dingy, and the food was bad. As he downed his unappetizing stew, Shannon thought nostalgically of the bright, friendly restaurant in Whiskey Creek where he had first met Kathy so long ago. "Best flapjacks in town," she had said. They were, too.

After finishing the uninspiring meal, Shannon made his way back up the street to the brick building with the sign above the door that said CITY MARSHAL. As he entered, a burly, middle-aged man looked up from the desk. The man was wearing a badge and holding a water glass full of whiskey.

"Who the devil are you?" he said, eyeing Shannon's heavy coat and half-hidden gun belt.

Shannon took his star out of his shirt and held it out.

"Clay Shannon, Whiskey Creek," he said.

"Whiskey Creek? You're a little bit out of your territory, ain't you?"

"Yes. Are you the marshal here?"

"Yeah. Josh Cooper. What're you doin' in Half Moon City?"

"Mind if I have a seat?" Shannon said, sinking into a chair.

"Sure, if you want," said Cooper. "I asked you a question."

Shannon explained his business. Cooper grunted.

"Sounds rough," he said, yawning. "Where you headed now?"

"I thought you might help me decide. Anybody pass through lately that might match their description?"

"Lotta people come through here, Shannon. The railroad brings 'em, the railroad takes 'em away. As long as they don't cause no trouble, I don't pay no attention to 'em."

"These men would have ridden in on horseback from the south," Shannon said. "Over the mountains. A couple of them might have been wounded."

Cooper shrugged.

"This here's an office, not a hospital," he said. "Anyway, I didn't see 'em. Maybe they pushed on."

"Perhaps," said Shannon. "But I've got reason to believe that one or more of them may still be in town."

"Maybe," Cooper grunted, taking another gulp of whiskey.

Shannon thought of Kathy's plea to him when he was leaving Whiskey Creek.

"There might be as many as six or eight of these people," he said. "If I locate them, any chance of getting a couple of your deputies to help me make the arrest?"

Marshal Cooper shook his head.

"Nope. This ain't my problem, Shannon. I got all I can do to take care of Half Moon City. If you need help, get it from your own county."

"Thanks for your courtesy," said Shannon, standing up and moving toward the door.

"I don't want you starting no trouble, understand?" Cooper called loudly. "That Whiskey Creek badge don't cut you no slack around here. Any gunplay in my town, you'll answer to me."

"I'll try to be good," Shannon said.

He left the marshal's office and walked slowly back to the hotel. There he entered his room and carefully locked the door behind him. He removed his saddlebags from the bed and slung them over a chair, then took the Winchester rifle and propped it in a corner near the bedstead. This done, he sat down wearily on the lumpy mattress to think. After the punishing ride over the mountains he was very tired, and the bed—lumps, squeaking springs, and all— beckoned invitingly to him. He thought of resisting the temptation to rest, of instead going back out into the streets to continue his search. But it was now growing late, and even if any of the outlaws were still in Half Moon City, the chances of locating them at night in a fair-sized town, without a clue as to their possible whereabouts, were slim. Grudgingly, he unbuckled his gun belt and hung it over the bedpost where he could reach it rapidly if the need arose. Then he stretched out on the bed, placed the Colt revolver beside him, and fell into a fitful sleep.

## Chapter Eight

Shannon was awakened by the sun streaming through the window of his room. He fumbled for his watch and blinked at it in dismay. It was already mid-morning. Chiding himself for his weakness in lying in bed so long when there was work to be done, Shannon arose, quickly washed and shaved, then buckled on his gun belt, locked the door behind him, and descended the hotel stairs.

The same clerk was still behind the lobby desk. He was sitting with his chair tipped back against the wall, dozing. Shannon rapped on the countertop to get the man's attention. The clerk sat upright, peering bleary-eyed at Shannon.

"I'm going out," Shannon said. "If a telegram comes for me while I'm gone, hold on to it and give it to me when I get back, will you?"

"I ain't no post office," the clerk grumbled. "I might not remember."

"Try," said Shannon.

"You gotta leave your key at the desk when you go out," said the desk clerk petulantly as Shannon started to leave. "I don't think so," said Shannon. "If I left it with you, somebody might be tempted to use it while I'm gone, and I wouldn't like that at all. Also, if there's an extra key around," he added, "you make sure nobody uses that one either. You *will* do that for me, won't you?"

The desk clerk frowned.

"Okay," he said sullenly. "I guess so."

"Sure you will," said Shannon under his breath as he left the hotel lobby.

Shannon ate a hasty breakfast at the dingy café and then went back down the hill to the telegraph office. The elderly telegrapher was there, hunched at his desk in front of the silent telegraph key.

"Any reply to my wire yet?" Shannon said.

"Nope," said the telegrapher. "Not yet. Must be important, huh?"

"Yes," said Shannon. "Very important."

"Well, maybe it'll come later today."

"I hope so," Shannon said.

He stopped by the livery stable to check on the buckskin, then began walking through the streets of Half Moon City, searching for some sign of the men he was after. *Perhaps they were never here*, he thought. *Or if they were here, they may have ridden on. But in that case, someone would have stayed to wait for the two bushwhackers they left behind. Probably just one man would have stayed, two at the most. Instead of a half-dozen or more, I may be looking for just one or two men. The trouble is, I don't even know which ones.*

As he walked, Shannon contemplated his alternatives. If the gang had indeed been in Half Moon City, then even if they had left there were a number of places in town where he still might obtain some information about their passing. He tried the general stores, thinking that the men might have gone in to buy supplies, but the storekeepers were unhelpful. Considering the possibility that someone's horse might have needed reshoeing after the trip over the rocky trail from Whiskey Creek, he stopped at the blacksmith shop. The smith looked at Shannon suspiciously as he made his inquiry, then continued hammering at a shoe he was forging.

"Nobody in here lately except regular customers," he said over the clanging of the hammer. "Sorry I can't help you." His tone indicated that if he was sorry, he was not exactly desolated. Shannon thanked him politely. Back on the main street, he asked for directions to the town doctor's office, and was told there were two in Half Moon City. There was no answer at the first office he tried, but at the second the door was opened by a small man wearing a stethoscope around his neck.

"What can I do fer you, young feller?" he said, sizing Shannon up. "You look healthy enough to me."

Shannon explained his errand, asking if any strangers had recently sought treatment for a gunshot wound.

"No," said the doctor, rubbing his chin reflectively, "haven't had anybody in here lately with lead in him. Delivered a couple of babies this week, and one of the saloon girls had to be patched up after she had a little disagreement with one of her associates, but that's all."

"What about the other doctor in town?" Shannon asked. "I knocked at his office, but there wasn't any answer. Would you know if he might have worked on a gunshot wound lately?"

"He might have," said the doctor with a wry smile, "but you're gonna have a hard time asking him. He died of a heart attack a couple of days ago. Just buried him yesterday morning."

Shannon thanked him and went back out onto the street. So far, everything was a dead end, one way or another. Now the best chance for a clue seemed to be the saloons in town, of which there were a large number. Men celebrating a success might have spent some time in one of them, bragging about their deeds. Furthermore, one or two men waiting for others might well have waited in a saloon. Indeed, they might still be waiting there.

He had no success at the first two saloons he checked. It was still early afternoon, and both establishments were almost empty. Later they would be crowded, and perhaps he would have better luck then.

As he approached the third saloon, a muscular man wearing a railroader's cap came stumbling out of the swinging doors and staggered down the steps into the street. As he did so, he cannoned into Shannon, nearly knocking both of them down. Shannon could smell the alcohol fumes on his breath.

"Sorry, friend," said Shannon, attempting to move around him.

The man backed off a step or two and glared belligerently at him.

"You ain't my friend," he rumbled, "and bein' sorry ain't enough. I'm gonna take you apart."

"I said I was sorry," Shannon said. "Why don't you just leave it at that?"

"Not a chance," the man said. He shouted an obscenity and charged at Shannon, swinging his fists wildly.

Shannon sidestepped and delivered a straight right to the man's jaw. The drunk dropped into the mud of the street and lay there, inert. After a moment or two, he began to snore.

A small crowd had come out of the saloon to see the fun. Shannon took the man by the shoulders and dragged him out of the middle of the street, propping him up against a handy water trough. The onlookers laughed and started to file back into the saloon. Shannon was about to follow them when Marshal Cooper came hurrying up, wiping his brow with a red bandanna.

"Shannon, I told you to stay out of trouble," he barked. "What did you do to this man?"

"Gave him what he deserved, Marshal," called one of the bystanders. "You know Frankie always gets mean when he drinks. The stranger was just defendin' himself."

"Well . . ." said Cooper, looking from the speaker to Shannon to the snoring drunk beside the water trough. "Okay, Shannon," he said sourly, "I'll let it go this time. But no more rough stuff in my town. Finish your business and ride on. Or else."

"I understand," Shannon said, carefully holding his temper. "By the way, have you remembered anything that might help me find the men I'm looking for?"

"No," said Cooper. "And if I had, I wouldn't bother to tell you." He swabbed his face with the bandanna again and walked away, grumbling to himself.

Shannon watched him go, suppressing his anger. Then he stepped up on the boardwalk to enter the saloon. As he did so, a young man wearing a deputy marshal's star touched his arm.

"I see you've met our beloved Marshal Cooper," he said with a twinkle in his eye.

"Yes," said Shannon. "I've had the dubious pleasure. Cheerful sort, isn't he? Pardon me, but I don't know your name."

"Fred Johnson," said the deputy, reaching out to shake hands. "I heard about what happened in your town and why you're here. I'm not sure, but I may be able to tell you something that might help you, if you're interested."

"I'm interested," Shannon said. "Buy you a drink?"

"Thanks," said the deputy. "That's mighty nice of you, considering the way you've been treated around here."

There were still only a few people in the saloon, and Shannon and Johnson found an empty table at the side of the room.

"Don't know whether this is anything useful," Johnson said, "but a bunch like the one you describe rode in just a few days ago. No idea where they come from, but they were tough-looking characters. You notice people like that when you're wearing a badge—you know what I mean. Anyway, they could've been the ones you're after, I reckon."

"Any of them wearing dusters?"

"No. Heavy coats, as I remember. But that's what you'd expect around here, with winter coming on."

Shannon nodded. The men he was seeking would undoubtedly have exchanged their dusters for heavier clothing as they encountered the colder temperatures of the mountains.

"Are these people still in Half Moon City?" Shannon asked.

"Don't believe so," Johnson said. "Saw them riding out of town day before yesterday. Don't think they came back. Blanket rolls on their saddles, like they were planning to be traveling for a while."

"Which way did they go?"

"North, into the high country. They could be anywhere up there by now."

"It doesn't matter," Shannon said. "I'll find them. There's no place they can go that's so high or so far or so deep that I won't find them."

"The thing is," Johnson said, "these may not even be the people you're looking for. Lots of hardcases come through here."

The nightmare flashed again through Shannon's mind.

"These men you saw—was one of them riding a pinto?"

Johnson thought for a moment.

"Yeah," he said, "there was a paint horse in the bunch. Don't see many of them around here. They're more common further up, toward Indian country."

"Did all of the men ride out?"

"Not quite. One of them's still here. The one riding the pinto, as a matter of fact. He's been hanging around the Golden Spur Saloon for the last couple of nights, getting drunk and looking unhappy. Might be there tonight, if you care to have a word with him."

Shannon's pulse quickened.

"Where's the Golden Spur?" he said.

"Next street over. Not much action during the day. Gets crowded after dark, though."

"What's this man look like?"

"Short, heavy build. Dark brown or black hair. Heavy coat, same as the others. Carries his holster slung low, like a gunfighter."

"I'll take a look," said Shannon, finishing his beer.

"No rush," said Johnson. "As far as I've noticed, he doesn't go in there until well after nightfall."

"That's several hours from now," Shannon said thoughtfully. "I'd like to find him sooner than that if I can, before he saddles up and follows his friends. Any idea where he might be holed up this time of the day?"

"Afraid not. Haven't seen him anywhere except in the saloon. Any of this useful to you?"

"Yes," said Shannon. "It definitely is. Thank you, Mr. Johnson. I appreciate your kindness."

"Glad to help," Johnson said. "I won't be able to go with you to look for him, though," he added apologetically. "Cooper's made it clear that none of the city deputies are to get involved with you."

Shannon smiled.

"You just did get involved," he said, rising. "And I'm very grateful. Don't worry, I won't tell Cooper you spoke with me."

They shook hands again.

"Good luck, Sheriff," said the deputy.

"I could use a little good luck," Shannon said. "For a change."

## Chapter Nine

Shannon went back to the hotel. He was still tired, and by the deputy's account there was no use looking for his man in the saloon until later in the evening. A couple of hours' more rest would help prepare him for whatever lay ahead. Soon he might be traveling again, and then there would be little time for resting. Entering the lobby, he approached the desk, where the same clerk was still behind the counter.

"Has my telegram come in from Whiskey Creek?" Shannon asked.

"Dunno," the clerk said indifferently. "Maybe, maybe not. Like I said, this ain't no post office."

Shannon reached over the counter, grabbed the desk clerk by the front of his shirt, and pulled him halfway across the top of the counter until the man's nose was an inch from his own.

"Mister," Shannon said, "I've had about enough of you.

I want a straight answer to my question and I want it *now*. Has there been a wire for me or not?"

"No sir," squeaked the clerk, his eyes wide. "Not a thing, sir. Honest. I'd know if there was, sir. Not a thing."

"I'm going upstairs for a while," Shannon said, twisting harder on the man's shirt. "If a message comes in for me, you'll come up and tell me about it *immediately,* won't you?"

"Yessir. I will, sir. Immediately!"

Shannon released the frightened man and went upstairs to his room. He felt slightly ashamed of himself for bullying the clerk, but he had to make certain that the wire, when it came, reached him without delay.

He lay down on the bed, but deeply tired though he was, sleep would not come. The gruesome images kept torturing him, images of blood and death, images of his weeping wife, images of his stricken child. Again and again he checked his watch, impatient for darkness to fall, anxious to begin what he hoped would be an evening rendezvous with one of the outlaws in the Golden Spur Saloon.

At length, as the sun dropped behind the mountain ranges and dusk began to creep over Half Moon City, Shannon arose. After splashing cold water in his face, he put on his hat, then carefully examined his six-gun to be sure it was fully loaded. He spun the cylinder to make certain that it was moving freely, then returned the weapon to its holster, hefting it several times to verify that the gun would come smoothly out of the leather if or when it was needed. Locking the door behind him, he gain descended the stairs to the lobby. The clerk popped up from his chair as Shannon approached.

"No wire yet, sir. Awfully sorry, sir."

"I'll be back," Shannon said. "If it comes in, don't forget to hold it for me."

"Oh, I will sir. I certainly will."

Shannon suppressed a smile and went out into the gathering dusk.

Once outside, Shannon headed directly for the Golden Spur Saloon. While he was still a block away, he could hear the notes of a tinny piano and the babble of voices coming from the place. *Just like the old days,* Shannon thought. *Walking into a saloon where everybody's drunk and everybody's carrying a gun. I'm getting too old for this.*

He pushed open the heavy glass-paneled door of the Golden Spur and went in. The atmosphere was filled with noise and tobacco smoke. The room was crowded, for it was a Saturday night and many of the denizens of Half Moon City had come to celebrate the end of their working week. Shannon eased over to the bar and beckoned to the bartender. He had to raise his voice to make himself heard over the hubbub, but no one was paying any attention to them anyway.

"I'm looking for a man who may be new in town," Shannon said. "Stocky man, dark hair, carries his six-gun slung low. I've heard he comes in here at night, stays a while, drinks quite a bit. Might be wearing a duster, might not. Anybody besides your regular customers hanging around during the past few days?"

The bartender averted his eyes and began wiping the bar with a dirty towel.

"Lots of new faces pass through this town, mister," he said. "Some go east, some go west, some don't go anywhere for a while. I don't take any notice. Healthier that way."

Shannon tossed a silver dollar on the bar.

"That'll buy you one drink of whiskey in this dive," said the bartender.

Shannon added a five-dollar gold piece. The bartender

scooped both coins into the pocket of his apron and looked around furtively.

"There's been a fella like that in here the last couple of nights," he said. "Haven't seen him around before. Wasn't wearing a duster, though. Winter coat, sheepskin, kinda beat up. Claims his name is Catlett. He sits at a corner table and drinks pretty steady, watchin' the doors. Said he was waitin' for someone. Didn't say who or why. Told me to tell him if anybody came in here lookin' for him. That's about it."

"Thanks," said Shannon. "I'll wait too. If he comes in, you needn't bother to let him know I was asking about him. Right?" He dropped another five-dollar gold piece on the bar.

"Gotcha," said the bartender. "I'll give you the high sign if I see him."

"Good," Shannon said. "Draw me a beer and keep the change."

Shannon found a table near the corner that the bartender had indicated and settled down to nurse his beer. Out of old habit he began committing the features of the saloon to memory, just in case the knowledge should later prove helpful. As he surveyed the room, he noted that the saloon had a side door in addition to the main entrance. Shannon had learned long ago that, for a lawman, a saloon's side or back door could be a lifesaving emergency exit or a source of deadly danger. In this case he would have to keep an eye on both doors, since Catlett might come in through either one. Or neither.

To pass the time, Shannon began to think about the man he had come to find. The name "Catlett" meant nothing to him, but it was probably an alias anyway. The description could have fit anyone, but it might also fit some of the people he was looking for. Were they still in town? The man the bartender described was alone, and he had said he was expecting someone. Was he waiting for the two gunmen that had stayed behind to ambush the posse? The dying bushwhacker had said something about "meet 'em later." Half Moon City would be as good a place as any for them to join up. Shannon sat back in his chair and slipped the rawhide thong off the hammer of the Colt.

As time passed, the beer grew warmer and Shannon started to become drowsy. The restless hours he had spent on the uncomfortable hotel bed were not enough to make up for the recent days and nights without sleep. He fought to stay alert.

A pendulum clock hung on the wall near him, its hands moving with infinite slowness around the dial. 10:00. 10:30. Perhaps no one would come. Or perhaps it would be the wrong man. Then what would he do? Try the grumpy marshal again? It didn't seem like a very promising solution.

The front door opened and a heavyset man walked in, glancing warily around the room as he made his way to the bar. His hat was pulled down, shadowing his face, and Shannon couldn't get a good look at his features in the dim light. However, his gun belt hung low on his hips and he was wearing a grimy sheepskin coat. Could this be the one? Shannon leaned forward in his chair, hoping.

The man said something to the bartender, who set a glass and a full bottle of whiskey in front of him. Shannon saw the bartender glance meaningfully in his direction as the man in the sheepskin coat picked up the bottle and left the bar. The newcomer wove his way through the crowd to a table in the corner. Someone was already sitting there, but the man with the bottle growled something at him, and the occupant of the table got up hastily and moved to another part of the room. The new arrival slumped into the chair nearest the wall, put the bottle on the table, and removed his hat, revealing his face for the first time. Shannon almost stopped breathing. It was the gunman who, five days earlier, had ridden his horse roughshod over Bobby Shannon's body as the boy lay helpless in the main street of Whiskey Creek.

The rage boiled up again in Shannon, and he started to rise from the table. Then a lifetime of experience came to his aid. Shannon was the consummate professional lawman, and he knew very well that this was no time to lose his objectivity or his temper. He sat back in his chair and sipped his beer, studying the gunman. The man's holster was slung far down on his right thigh, and the bottom of the holster was tied down tightly to his leg. In addition, the leather thong was looped securely around the hammer of the six-gun. This would make it difficult for him to draw the weapon quickly from a sitting position. But when he did draw the gun he would probably be proficient with it. This was an experienced killer, not some first-time stickup man. Shannon would have to be careful. He looked carefully around the room to see if any other member of the gang might be in the saloon, but all of the people there were strangers to him. The minutes ticked slowly by, and although Catlett's eyes wandered repeatedly toward the doors, Shannon saw no sign that he recognized anyone who came in. The outlaw was apparently still alone, still waiting.

Shannon reached inside his coat, slipped the star out of his shirt pocket, and unobtrusively pinned it on. Then he got up and walked slowly toward the corner where Catlett was seated. The gunman paid no attention to him until he was standing right in front of the table. Holding his arms loosely at his sides, Shannon looked down into the man's eyes.

"You're under arrest, Catlett," he said.

"What?" said Catlett, startled. "I ain't done nothing! Who are you, anyway?"

"You know my name," Shannon said. "You and I met a

few days ago in a place called Whiskey Creek. Remember?"

Catlett's eyes widened in recognition.

"Shannon!" he said. "How did you...."

"Never mind how. Just stand up, nice and slow. And keep your hands where I can see them. We're going to take a stroll down to the city marshal's office. You and I need to have a little talk."

Catlett stared unbelievingly at him for another moment, then slowly started to rise. When he was halfway to his feet, he suddenly reached for his six-gun. Shannon kicked the table into his stomach, knocking him backward. He hit the wall hard and fell to the floor, gasping for breath. His hand again moved toward his holster. Instantly Shannon covered him with the Colt.

"Don't do it, mister," he said. "I want you alive, but I'll take you dead if I have to."

Catlett's eyes narrowed.

"You wouldn't kill me right here," he said. "Not in front of all these people." He gestured around the room. The crowd had fallen silent, and everyone in the saloon was staring at them.

"Naw," said Catlett, "you won't shoot me. You got too many witnesses."

"Try me," said Shannon, pressing the muzzle of his six-gun into Catlett's stomach. There was a wild, deadly glitter in Shannon's eyes, and Catlett turned pale, realizing that the man with the star meant exactly what he said.

"Okay, okay," Catlett cried. "Just take it easy. I ain't gonna draw against the drop."

Shannon lifted the outlaw's revolver from its holster and tucked it into his belt.

"Stand up," he said, "and put your hands behind you."

Catlett complied, and Shannon stepped behind him, took a pair of handcuffs out of his coat pocket, and clamped them on the gunman's wrists. "Now," Shannon said, "start toward the door. *Slowly.* If you try to run, I'll kill you before you get ten feet."

He herded the outlaw through the silent crowd toward the front door.

"Hey, mister," said someone, "what do you think you're doing? You ain't the law here!"

"Yeah, somebody stop him," someone else yelled. Several of the people in the room edged forward, trying to block the path to the door.

"Catlett," Shannon said in a loud voice, "if anyone tries to interfere, I'll kill you, and them too if I have to. I've already pulled the trigger on this six-gun, so only my thumb is holding back the hammer. Even if somebody shoots me in the back, I'll still get you before I go down."

"Don't try nothin', you people!" Catlett squawked. "He'll do it!"

"Aw, let 'em go," said a man standing at the bar. "None of our business anyway."

There was a murmur of agreement from the crowd, and those who had started forward now stepped back, clearing the way. Shannon pushed Catlett through the swinging doors and into the street. The cold air felt good, and Shannon breathed deeply, thankful to be alive.

As they left the saloon, Shannon checked the hitchrack. A pinto was tied to it, the same one whose memory had been etched in Shannon's mind since Whiskey Creek. Well, the horse would keep. Meanwhile there were things to be done.

None too gently, Shannon prodded Catlett along the boardwalk with the barrel of his revolver. In the darkness, no one paid any attention to them. As they passed the mouth of an alley, Shannon grabbed Catlett by the collar and pushed him back into the shadows.

"Hey," said Catlett, "What're you—"

Shannon slammed him into a wall and shoved the muzzle

of the Colt up under his chin. A square of light from a
nearby window illuminated the man's startled face.
"Where's the rest of your gang?" Shannon said harshly.
"Where did they go?"
"I dunno what yer talkin' about," Catlett wheezed. His
eyes were crossed as he tried to look down at the gun barrel
close under his jaw. Shannon pressed the muzzle a little
harder into Catlett's throat.
"Don't give me that, you weasel," Shannon said. "I've
got an account to settle with you, and if I have to I'll do
it right here in this alley. Nothing would give me greater
pleasure than to splatter you all over this wall. Now *talk!*"
"I don't know nothin' about no gang. I wuz just waitin'
here for a coupla friends of mine."
"They aren't coming, Catlett. They're dead. And you're
going to be dead too in about thirty seconds if you don't
tell me what I want to know. Now, where are the rest of
them?"
"Who?" Catlett gurgled. "I told you I don't know nothin'
about—"
Shannon pressed still harder with the Colt, raising Ca-
tlett's chin up high and lifting him onto his tiptoes. Catlett
squawked in pain.
"Okay, okay," he said. "They rode on."
"Drago too?"
"Yeah, all of 'em."
"Where were you going to join them?"
"Cabin on the trail, beyond the next range. Log cabin.
Just over a stream, in some big fir trees. About forty miles.
They said we couldn't miss it."
"Who's 'we'? You and the two men you were supposed
to meet here?"
"Yeah. You, uh, you say you killed them?"
"Yes. With great pleasure. The same pleasure I'm going
to take in killing you if you give me any trouble. Now walk

in front of me out of the alley and turn left. For now, you've got a date with a jail cell. Later you've got a date with the hangman."

He removed the barrel of the Colt from beneath Catlett's chin. Catlett rubbed his throat, glaring resentfully at Shannon.

"I'll get you for this," he said.

Shannon rammed the gun barrel into Catlett's stomach.

"You're welcome to try," Shannon said. "It'll give me a good excuse. Now *move!*"

A few moments later, Shannon propelled his prisoner firmly through the door of the city marshal's office. Fred Johnson, the deputy city Marshall, was sitting at the desk. Marshal Cooper was nowhere in sight.

"Where's Cooper?" Shannon said, keeping his six-gun pointed at Catlett's back.

"Gone out for a drink, Sheriff," said the deputy, getting to his feet. "Be back later. This your man?"

"Yes, this is him," Shannon replied. "Not much to look at, is he? Just your average coward, thief, and murderer."

Johnson grinned.

"You taking him with you now, or do you want me to lock him up?"

"I'd appreciate it if you'd lock him up for a while," Shannon said. "The charges are robbery, kidnapping, and murder—about a dozen counts. I'll be going after his friends first, but later I'll take this coyote and anyone else I can catch back to Whiskey Creek to stand trial. Can you keep him behind bars for me until then?"

"No problem," Johnson said. "When are you heading out after the rest of then?"

"Tomorrow morning," said Shannon, tossing Johnson the key to the handcuffs. "Meanwhile I have some things to do. I'll be back here later tonight to talk to this skunk.

There are a few more questions I want to ask him before I start for the mountains."

Johnson picked the cell keys off their hook and took Catlett by the arm. Shannon holstered his six-gun.

"Catlett," he said, "where's your horse?"

"If you're so smart, go find it yourself," Catlett said sulkily.

"Couldn't be that pinto I saw hitched outside the Golden Spur on our way out of there, could it?"

Catlett frowned and looked away.

"Thought so," said Shannon. "Thanks. You've been very helpful."

## Chapter Ten

Shannon watched as Catlett was locked in one of the cells, then left the office and retraced his route back to the Golden Spur Saloon. The pinto was still tied to the hitch rack. Deftly Shannon searched the saddlebags, but there was no money. All he found was the usual collection of items carried by any rider while traveling, plus an extra six-gun tucked away in the bottom of one of the pouches and a small deerskin bag decorated with colored beads. The bag was empty. Shannon inspected it carefully, then slipped it into his pocket.

He stepped onto the boardwalk and looked through the glass panels of the saloon's front door, scrutinizing the faces inside the smoky room. There was still no one in the place that looked familiar to him. He moved back into the shadows of the covered walk and took up a position across from the corner of the saloon building, where he could see both the front and side doors of the Golden Spur. He leaned against the wall and watched, but after nearly an hour no one had entered or left the saloon whom he could identify. Perhaps, as Catlett claimed, the others had all ridden on. Well, he would have a talk with Catlett in his cell; there, unlike the alley, there would be no danger of being interrupted by curious passersby. Perhaps the gunman could be persuaded to tell him more about the raid on Whiskey Creek and the men who had carried it out.

Shannon untied the pinto from the hitch rail in front of the saloon and led the horse down to the livery stable. After turning the animal over to the night man, he checked again on the buckskin, then hurried back up the street to the city marshal's office.

When he entered the office, Marshal Cooper was seated at the desk counting some gold coins. The deputy, Fred Johnson, was leaning against the far wall looking disgruntled. Shannon nodded to him, then spoke to Cooper.

" 'Evening, Marshal," he said. "I'd like to spend a little time with my prisoner, if you don't mind."

"Prisoner?" said Cooper, rolling a cigarette. "Oh, him. He's gone."

Shannon stared at him. For a moment he thought he might have misunderstood.

"Gone?" he said. "How could he be *gone?*"

"Posted bail," said Cooper blandly. He stuck the cigarette in his mouth and lighted it.

Shannon took three steps forward and leaned over the desk, his face close to Cooper's.

"That man was under arrest, Cooper. He was my prisoner. He was supposed to be held here until I could take him back to Whiskey Creek for trial. How could he have made *bail?*"

"Posted a hundred dollars' bond," said Cooper, indicating the coins on the desk. "What was I supposed to do?"

"Hold him, you nitwit!" Shannon shouted. He looked

over at Johnson. "What happened here?" he demanded. Johnson shook his head in disgust.

"Catlett gave the marshal a hundred dollars," he said, "and the marshal let him go. That's the way things work around here."

"Shut up, Johnson," said Cooper. "Go wait outside until I'm through here."

The deputy cast a disdainful look at Cooper and left, slamming the door behind him.

Shannon looked at the money on the desk.

"That's not 'bail,' is it, Cooper?" he said angrily. "That's a bribe, isn't it? You took a bribe to let a murderer go."

Cooper shrugged.

"Gotta make a living," he said. "I expect you've done the same in your time."

Shannon's face was hard. His eyes were even harder.

"No," he said, "I have *not* 'done the same.' Ever."

"Then you're a fool," Cooper said, pocketing the coins.

Shannon walked around the desk toward Cooper. The marshal came to his feet, a look of sudden apprehension on his face. Without a word, Shannon reached up and tore the badge off Cooper's shirt. Cooper gaped at him, his face reddening. Shannon's voice shook with indignation as he held the badge up under Cooper's nose.

"You aren't fit to wear this," he said. "You're a disgrace to every decent lawman who ever carried a star. You make me want to vomit." He slammed the badge down on the desktop. The pin on the back of the badge broke off and went bouncing onto the floor.

Cooper's features twisted in wrath. His right hand dropped to the butt of his revolver and he started to draw. Shannon clamped his left hand down on Cooper's wrist with a grip of iron.

"Don't try it, Cooper," he hissed. "You aren't good enough."

Cooper hesitated, measuring Shannon's stare, then dropping his eyes toward Shannon's right hand as it hovered near his holster. After a few seconds, discretion got the better of Cooper's ire. He let go of the gun butt, pulled away from Shannon, and sat down in his chair.

"Get out of here, mister," he said in a low voice, avoiding Shannon's eyes. "Get out of here while you still can. If you're in this town an hour from now, I'll come after you with a dozen deputies and turn you into dog meat."

"You couldn't pay me enough to stay around any longer than I have to," Shannon said. "But I'll leave when I'm ready, whether it's now or an hour from now or a week from now. As it happens, at the moment I'm waiting for a telegram. When I have it, I'll ride out. In the meantime, if you feel like trying your luck, with or without your deputies, I'll be at the hotel, ready to entertain you."

He turned his back contemptuously on Cooper and walked out the door, wondering if the marshal would shoot him from behind before he reached the sidewalk.

The deputy, Fred Johnson, was standing outside. When Shannon closed the door, Johnson walked over to him, shaking his head.

"I apologize for that, Shannon," he said. "Cooper's crooked as a snake. There's a rumor that he did a stretch in Yuma prison before he came north to take up marshaling. Anyway, this isn't the first payoff he's taken. He'd sell his mother for twenty dollars."

"Why do you work for a man like that?"

"Somebody's got to enforce the law in this town," Johnson said. "The rest of us do what we can. As for his threats, he doesn't have a dozen deputies. There's only myself and two others. We won't help him against you, and he's just proved he hasn't got the guts to face you alone. In addition to being a crook, he's also got a yellow streak a mile wide."

"That kind can still be dangerous," Shannon said.

"Yes," said Johnson, "but if he comes at you, chances are it'll be from behind. Watch your back."

"That's good advice," Shannon said. "I'll keep it in mind."

"And remember," Johnson added, "if I can help you with anything, let me know."

"Thanks," Shannon said. "I appreciate the offer, but as soon as I get my telegram, I'll be on my way."

He shook hands with the deputy and hurried back to the livery stable. The pinto that Catlett had been riding was still there. The night stableman was a bent old man who hardly looked strong enough to walk, let alone shovel out a stall.

"Anybody come around looking for that pinto?" Shannon asked him.

"No sir, not a soul."

"Put him out of sight somewhere," Shannon said. "Rear stall, maybe. And if anyone does ask, tell 'em you never saw any such horse, will you?"

The stable man looked dubious.

"I don't want to get into trouble with nobody," he said, scowling.

Shannon dropped a silver dollar into his hand.

"That affect your memory any?" he said.

"Yes, sir!" the man said, grinning broadly. "Somebody asks, I don't know nothing about no paint horse."

"Good," said Shannon. "I'll be back in the morning for him."

Shannon walked back to the hotel, musing about the pinto. Catlett must have left town on someone else's horse. Stole one, probably. Shannon found himself hoping that the horse Catlett had stolen was Marshal Cooper's.

As Shannon entered the hotel, the desk clerk straightened up and looked at him apprehensively.

"My wire come yet?"

"No, sir. Honest. Nothing at all."

"I'll be in my room. You'll tell me when it comes, won't you?"

"Oh, yes, Mr. Shannon. I'll tell you the minute it comes in. Really I will."

"I have every confidence in you," Shannon said as he climbed the stairs.

## Chapter Eleven

Shannon woke with the dawn. He splashed some water on his face from the pitcher that stood on the nightstand, then took out his razor and began to shave. He had just finished wiping the soap off his face and was returning his meager belongings to his saddlebags when there was a knock on the door. *Good*, he thought, *maybe it's the answer to my wire about Bobby.* With his six-gun in his hand, Shannon stepped to one side of the door and called out, "Yes? Who is it?"

"Let me in, Clay," said a familiar voice.

Shannon gasped in surprise. He holstered the Colt and unlocked the door. Pedro Rodriguez stood in the hallway, a thin smile on his weatherbeaten face.

"Pete!" Shannon said. "Come in, man, come in!" The warmth in his voice was heartfelt. Rodriguez had been his deputy when Shannon was taming Whiskey Creek, and during that time he had saved Shannon's life more than once. He had left Whiskey Creek two years previously to take a

job as marshal of Dry Wells, a town some miles to the
south. Shannon had not seen him in over a year. Pete Rodriguez was a good lawman and a good friend, and Shannon,
loner though he was, was genuinely glad to see him now.

"What are you doing here?" he said, after they had
shaken hands and Rodriguez had seated himself in the
room's only chair.

"Your wife got a message to me in Dry Wells, asking
me to come to Whiskey Creek," he said. "I got there two
days ago. She told me what had happened, and asked me
to come after you, to aid you in any way I could. She said
you needed help and wouldn't accept it from anyone but
me."

"I asked her not to bother you," Shannon said, sitting
down on the edge of the bed. "But it's good to see you
again. Very good."

Rodriguez nodded.

"Yes," he said. "It is a great pleasure to see you also."

Shannon realized for the first time that Rodriguez's face
was haggard, and there was a haunted look in his eyes. It
occurred to Shannon that to reach Half Moon City so soon,
Rodriguez must have ridden very hard indeed through the
mountains, even harder than had Shannon himself.

"I sent Kathy a wire to ask about Bobby," Shannon said,
"but I haven't gotten a reply yet. Did you see him when
you were in Whiskey Creek? How is he?"

Rodriguez dropped his gaze. His face suddenly looked
not only tired but very old.

"I bring you very bad news, Clay," he said. "Bobby's
dead. He died the day I arrived in Whiskey Creek."

"Dead?" Shannon said. "My son is dead? But my
wire . . ."

"Señora Shannon got your wire that same day, but decided not to answer it. She did not like to keep Bobby's
death from you, but she felt it would be better if I told you

in person when I got here. She knew you'd take it hard, and she wanted a friend to be with you when you heard about it. I am truly sorry, amigo. I know how much you loved the boy."

Shannon got up and walked to the window. He stood there for a long while, looking out at the sun rising over the nearby peaks. When at last he spoke, his voice was thick and strained.

"Did he ever recover consciousness?" he said.

"No," Rodriguez replied. "He never woke up. He just slipped away, quietly. One minute he was breathing, the next minute he was gone. The doctor and your wife were with him. Señora Shannon said it was a mercy that the child never knew what had happened to him."

"How's Kathy taking it?" Shannon asked.

"Badly," said Rodriguez, "but in a very strange way. I swear to you, amigo, I've never seen her like that. She just sat there looking at his body for a long time, without saying a word. No tears, nothing. It was as if her soul had turned to stone."

"Poor Kathy," Shannon murmured. "I should have been there."

"Do not blame yourself, amigo. There was nothing you could have done."

"When was the funeral?"

"He was to be buried the next day. Forgive me, my friend, but I did not stay for the service. By then I was on the way here. It was Señora Shannon's wish that I start out immediately to find you."

Shannon pressed his forehead against the glass of the window and closed his eyes.

"Thank you for telling me, Pete," he said. "Kathy was right. I'd rather hear it from you than from some telegraph office. Or some miserable little desk clerk." He turned around to face Rodriguez. The morning light was now

flooding the room, and Rodriguez could see that Shannon's
eyes were dry, empty, and as cold as ice. A chill went
through Rodriguez, for he saw death in those eyes.
"What will you do now, Clay?" Rodriguez asked, a little
shaken. "I will ride back to Whiskey Creek with you if you
like."
There was a long pause.
"I'm not going back just yet," Shannon said finally.
"There's nothing more I can do there now. I'm going into
the high timberland to find the men who killed my boy and
Billy Joe and Mayor Ford and all the rest, and caused my
wife and my town so much pain."
"*Bueno*," Rodriguez said. "That is settled then. Señora
Shannon told me you were tracking the gang, and we knew
from your wire that you had come here to Half Moon City.
That is all I know. What has happened since then?"
Shannon walked back to the bed and began to finish
packing his saddlebags.
"I caught up with one of them in a saloon here, a man
named Catlett. He was waiting for the two drygulchers I
shot in the hills outside Whiskey Creek. He said the rest
of them were on their way to some sort of line shack in
the mountains. Before I had a chance to get anything else
out of him, the corrupt marshal of this so-called city let
him go. By now, Catlett's probably well on his way there
too."
"Well, then, amigo," said Rodriguez, "we should get
started, no?"
"I don't want you to come with me, Pete. I thank you
for the offer and for your friendship, but I don't want your
wife to be a widow because you tried to help me. Catlett
probably high-tailed it out of town last night as soon as he
was turned loose, and when he joins up with the rest of the
gang he'll tell them what happenend here. Then they'll
know I'm coming after them, and they'll be up there some-

where, waiting. They could pick us off easily on those mountain trails. We'd be sitting ducks. No, too many people have died already because of my stupidity. I don't want your death on my conscience as well."

"I am going with you Clay," Rodriguez said firmly. "I promised Señora Shannon I would. And even if I had not made that promise, I would go anyway for the sake of our friendship. Come on, *compadre*. It will be just like the old days."

"We survived the old days, Pete," Shannon replied. "We might not survive this. We could die together up there in those mountains."

"Then we will die in good company, my friend," Rodriguez said. "No man could ask for more."

## Chapter Twelve

Despite Rodriguez's protests to the contrary, it was obvious to Shannon that the man was badly fatigued after his rapid journey from Whiskey Creek, so he insisted that Rodriguez remain in the hotel room and get a little rest while Shannon made the preparations for their departure.

"My horse is very tired also," Rodriguez said. "I asked much of her riding over from Whiskey Creek, and it would not be wise to take a worn-out animal into the mountains again. I think I will have to leave her here and find another."

"I'll get you one," said Shannon. "Tell me what you want, and I'll find it."

"You choose," said Rodriguez. "I trust your judgment— about horses and about men."

"Another thing," Shannon said. "We're going to have to carry a fair load of supplies with us. No general stores where we're going, and we don't know how long we may be out there. What about taking a pack animal along?"

"*Bueno*," Rodriguez said. "It will allow us to carry more and ease the burden on our own horses."

"I'll take care of that, too. Your horse tied up in front of the hotel?"

"Yes. A bay mare."

"I'll see to her. Back in an hour, hour and a half at the most."

"Then I will take a little siesta," said Rodriguez, testing the mattress. "Or at least I will try. What is in this bed? I've slept on rocks that were softer."

As he left the hotel, Shannon met the deputy marshal, Fred Johnson, walking along the street. They exchanged greetings, and then Shannon said casually, "By the way, did anybody report a horse stolen last night?"

Johnson gave him a puzzled look.

"No, not to me," he said. "Someone might have told Cooper or one of the other deputies about it. Why do you ask?"

"Just wondering," Shannon said. If Catlett had not stolen a horse, and had not reclaimed the pinto Shannon had hidden away in the livery stable, how did the outlaw get out of town? Perhaps the answer was that he didn't leave town after all. He could be hiding out somewhere in Half Moon City, lying low until Shannon had gone. The thought nagged at Shannon, but he put it aside. Surely, Catlett must have fled for the mountains as soon as he was released. Flight would do him little good, however; Shannon would catch up to him sooner or later.

Shannon untied Rodriguez's mare from the hitch rail in front of the hotel and led it down toward the livery stable. The animal walked slowly, with its head down.

"Poor old girl," Shannon said, rubbing the mare's neck. "You've come a long way. Well, you'll get a little vacation now while somebody else does the work."

Shannon led the mare into the livery barn. The owner was there, pitching hay for his boarders.

"Anybody try to collect that pinto I brought in here last night?" Shannon asked.

"Guess not," the owner said. "Night man didn't say anything about it, and the critter is still back there in one of the rear stalls, eatin' like a hog. Is there a problem?"

"No," said Shannon. "At least I hope not."

He explained to the livery stable owner that he wanted to board the mare and obtain another mount for Rodriguez. The livery owner took him to the rear of the building and showed him several horses in his corral.

"That big sorrel looks good," Shannon said. "How much is he?"

"Smart choice," said the stable owner approvingly. "That's one tough horse. The former owner rode it in here over the mountains through the snowstorm they had up there a couple of weeks ago. The rider died of pneumonia, but the horse was fine."

The stableman named his price; it was fair, and Shannon did not haggle.

"I'll need a pack animal, too," he said. "Got any pack horses or mules?"

" 'Fraid not," said the other man. "But what about the pinto you was just talkin' about? Looks like a sturdy sort. Not much for riding, I'd say, but might make a good pack horse."

Shannon considered this. The animal was Catlett's, not his, but Catlett had left it behind. *Might be neighborly to take it along and return it to him*, Shannon thought wryly.

Shannon inspected the pinto carefully to make certain that it was sound.

"Should do," he decided. "Got any pack saddles?"

"Sure," said the stable owner. "People use 'em a lot around here. Make you a good deal on one."

They completed the arrangements and Shannon paid the agreed-upon price. He told the livery owner that he would be back shortly for the pack horse, and soon after that for the buckskin and the sorrel.

"What about the riding saddle that was on the pinto?" said the livery man.

"If somebody named Catlett comes looking for it, give it to him," Shannon said. "Otherwise, keep it as a present from me."

Shannon next went to the telegraph office and wrote out another message. The telegrapher read through it carefully, counting the words.

" 'Kathy Shannon, Whiskey Creek. Rodriguez here. Told me about Bobby. Pete going with me into mountains after gang. Don't worry. I love you. Clay.' That it?"

"Yes," said Shannon tersely.

"Who's Bobby?" the old man asked, peering at Shannon through his thick spectacles.

Shannon looked away.

"Nobody," he said. "Not anymore."

"Excuse me, mister," said the telegrapher hastily. "Didn't mean to get personal. Say, you're still under twenty-five words. Anything to add?"

"No," said Shannon. "That says it all, unfortunately."

Shannon stopped in at the livery and collected the pinto. He placed the pack saddle on the animal and then, taking the horse's lead, he walked him up toward the large mercantile store that stood just beyond the stable.

In the general store, Shannon made his purchases. He bought flour and bacon and beans and coffee, a good two weeks' supply, together with extra blankets, matches, and other items.

"If you're going into the mountains this time of year, you're going to need a heavier coat than the one you have on," the storekeeper said. Shannon frowned. The man was right. The coats he and Rodriguez were wearing were enough for the mild winters of Whiskey Creek and its surrounding country, but they would not be enough here. He bought two, guessing at Rodriguez's size. As he was piling his selections on the store counter, he happened to glance through the open door of the storeroom nearby. Some wooden cases were stacked there, and one of them was open, revealing its contents.

"I'll take six of those sticks of dynamite," Shannon said.

"Six? You want blasting caps and some fuse, too?"

"Yes."

"Land sakes, Sheriff," said the storekeeper. "What do you need that stuff for? Only railroad men and miners use it around here. You going prospecting for gold?"

"Not gold," said Shannon. "Rattlesnakes."

He paid for the goods, and then began to carry them out to load them on the pack horse. As he stepped into the street with the flour and bacon piled in his arms, a shout from behind him froze him in his tracks.

"Turn around, Shannon," said the voice. "I'm gonna kill ya, and I want ya to die lookin' straight at me!"

Shannon turned. The outlaw, Catlett, was standing on the boardwalk not twenty feet away, and he had a rifle aimed at Shannon's chest. The rifle was cocked, and Catlett's finger was on the trigger. With his arms full of supplies, Shannon knew he had no chance of reaching his own gun before Catlett could put a bullet in his heart.

He cursed himself for his lack of caution. He had supposed that Catlett had left town. What was it he had said to Mayor Ford back in Whiskey Creek? *When you carry a star, you can't afford to assume anything.* And he had made just exactly that mistake. He had known it was not certain that Catlett had left Half Moon City, but he had assumed that such was the case. Now the assumption had proven disastrously wrong, and Shannon was trapped, helpless, about to pay the price for his own unforgivable error. And that price would be paid soon, for he could see that Catlett was already squeezing the trigger of the rifle. In the instant he had left to him, Shannon thought: *What a silly way to die, standing in the middle of the street with my arms full of groceries.*

Catlett fired. The impact of the bullet knocked Shannon backward into the dirt. He staggered to his feet, his senses still reeling. There was flour all over him, but surprisingly no blood. Seeing the torn bag of flour lying on the ground beside his other purchases, Shannon immediately understood—the bullet had buried itself in the flour bag, expending its force in the flour. The slug had never reached Shannon's body.

Catlett was cocking the rifle for another shot, but now Shannon was no longer impeded by the supplies he had been holding. He drew his revolver and fired. The bullet hit Catlett low in the chest. Dust flew from his shirt. He grunted and staggered against the wall of the building beside him. Then he crumpled onto the dusty boards of the sidewalk.

Shannon ran toward the fallen man and kicked the rifle out of reach, but there was no need. The outlaw had no more fight left in him. Shannon knelt beside him to examine the wound. Catlett was moving feebly, trying to speak, but it was obvious that he did not have long to live.

Curious onlookers were gathering around, attracted by the shots.

"One of you people get a doctor," Shannon said, starting to get to his feet.

"Don't move, Shannon," someone said loudly. Shannon looked up and found Marshal Cooper standing above him, covering him with a six-gun. There was a look of malignant glee on Cooper's face.

"You're under arrest, Shannon," he said happily. "You'll swing for this, I swear it. Drop your gun."

Deputy Marshal Fred Johnson came running up.

"Hold it, Cooper," he said. "Catlett fired first. Shannon acted in self-defense."

"Don't give me that," said Cooper. "I saw it all, and it was just plain murder. I'm takin' Shannon in. Now drop that gun, Shannon, or I'll drop you."

"Just a moment, Marshal," said a well-dressed elderly man who was pushing his way through the crowd. "I saw it all too, and Deputy Johnson is correct. This man you call Shannon fired in self-defense. No court in the land would convict him. What are you trying to pull here, anyway?"

"You stay out of this, Judge," Cooper growled. "We ain't in court now."

Catlett opened his eyes. He peered around feebly and his gaze fell upon Cooper.

"Sorry, Cooper," he wheezed. "I tried to get him like you said, but he was too fast."

"Shut your face, Catlett," Cooper snarled. "You don't know what you're talkin' about."

Shannon bent over Catlett again.

"Catlett," he said, "did Cooper pay you to kill me?"

"Yeah," said Catlett. "Said to get you from behind. Said—"

Cooper shot the dying outlaw between the eyes. The watching crowd stumbled back, dumbfounded at the stark brutality of the act. Cooper was already turning toward Shannon, cocking his revolver for another shot. Shannon sprang at Cooper and swung his Colt in a sharp, short arc that connected solidly with Cooper's skull. The marshal collapsed onto the sidewalk, holding his head and moaning. His six-gun clattered to the walk beside him. Shannon seized it and tossed it aside.

"You pitiful little toad," he said, looking down at Cooper

as the marshal struggled to sit up. "You didn't have the sand to face me, so you hired this two-bit backshooter to do your dirty work for you."

"You can't prove that," Cooper said, looking up, his face defiant.

"We don't have to prove it, Cooper," said the judge. "We all saw you kill that man in cold blood. A dying man, defenseless, and you deliberately killed him to stop him from talking. You're through in Half Moon City, Cooper. I want your badge, and I want it now."

Cooper got painfully to his feet.

"You can't take my badge," he said. "I got friends in this town. . . ."

"Josh," said the deputy, Fred Johnson, "you ain't got a friend in the world, much less in this town. And Judge Peyton is right—you're through here. Get on your horse and ride out right now, or I'll arrest you for murder."

"And I'll hang him for it," said the judge. "The badge, Cooper. Now."

His face still pale from the shock of the blow from the barrel of Shannon's Colt, Cooper reached into his pocket and produced the badge, sullenly handing it to the judge. Then he stooped over to pick up his revolver.

"Let it lie!" said Shannon.

Cooper gave him one final look of hatred and then went stumbling away up the walk, swaying and holding his aching head.

"I'll see to it he gets out of town, Shannon," Deputy Johnson said. "We don't want him taking another crack at you before you go on your way. Say, did you ever get that message you were waiting for?"

"Yes," said Shannon, "I got it. I can leave now. Let me know which direction Cooper takes, will you?"

"Sure," said Johnson. "What a pleasure it's going to be not to have him around anymore."

"Once again, justice triumphs," said Judge Peyton, looking smug. Shannon thought of his murdered child, and of all the other innocent people he had seen lying dead and wounded in the streets of Whiskey Creek and in the hills beyond it.

"You're wrong, Judge," Shannon said. "Justice never triumphs, because it always comes too late."

## Chapter Thirteen

Shannon and Rodriguez mounted their horses, and with Rodriguez holding the lead line of the pack animal they started out on their manhunt. As they passed the city marshal's office, Fred Johnson came out the door. Shannon reined up and introduced Johnson to Rodriguez.

"Proud to meet you, Marshal," Johnson said. He grinned at Shannon. "I'm a marshal too, now," he said. "They gave me Cooper's job."

Shannon leaned down to shake hands.

"Congratulations," he said. "And my sympathies."

Johnson laughed.

"Thanks," he said. "I know what you mean. I've got to get a new badge, though—you busted Cooper's last night. Come to think of it, I guess you busted Cooper, too."

"Did you see Cooper leave?" Shannon asked. He had vowed to make no more assumptions.

"Took the north road," Johnson said. "Went out of here like ten thousand devils were chasing him."

"What kind of horse?"

"Gray gelding, kind of bony. Cooper never fed him much. Won't last long in those mountains."

"Any idea where Cooper might be headed?"

"None. Not much up there except the U.S. Army post at Little Gap, and the Wind River Indian Agency the other side of the Kimasee range."

"And the cabin Catlett said was the rendezvous point," Shannon mused. "Do you know if Catlett told Cooper about that?"

"Don't know for sure. Could be, though. You think Cooper might throw in with the people you're after?"

"Stranger things have happened," Shannon said. "Cooper's out of a job, he's a convicted felon, he's already done business with Catlett, and he's nursing a big grudge against me." He looked meaningfully at Rodriguez. "If Catlett told Cooper where he was supposed to meet Drago, and Cooper decides to join up with Drago and tells him what he knows about us, we may be sitting ducks after all. Drago and his bunch will know we're coming after them."

Rodriguez shrugged.

"No matter," he said. "We will find them anyway."

"Yes," Shannon replied. "Unless they find us first."

They bid good-bye to Half Moon City's new marshal and headed out of town. Not long after they left the last cluster of buildings behind, the road narrowed and began to rise sharply. Rodriguez peered up at the peaks rising above them.

"I do not know this country at all," he said. "Marshal Johnson mentioned an army fort and an Indian agency, I think?"

"Yes. Wind River reservation, over the second range. The army post is a good thirty or forty miles further on. Fort Arthur. Small place—just a single cavalry troop, I'm told."

"Where do you think this Drago fellow is planning to go?"

Shannon considered. The outlaws would be unlikely to go near a military post, but they might head for the Indian reservation. He remembered the beaded deerskin bag he had found among Catlett's belongings. He reached back into his saddle bag and brought it out to show Rodriguez.

"What do you make of it?" said Rodriguez. "Is the design something the Wind River Indians use?"

"I don't know," Shannon said. "I'm not familiar with the artwork of the tribes in this part of the world. But I don't believe in coincidences very much. I'd say the odds are good that the bag came from that reservation. Whether the Drago gang got it there or just stole it from someone who had been there is anybody's guess."

He put the bag away.

"At any rate, it suggests that Drago's bunch might have been to the Wind River reservation before, and if that's so they could go back to it. I don't think they will, though. Not now, not when they're on the run. No, the likelihood is they're planning to avoid any more populated areas and just make themselves scarce in some hideout in one of those high valleys. Not many people up there, and no law at all. Just what they'd want. A hundred men could look for a hundred years and never find them in that country."

"We will find them," Rodriguez said firmly.

Following this exchange, Shannon and Rodriguez said little as they rode. They were both essentially silent men, used to speaking only when necessary and then saying only what was necessary. At one point Shannon asked Rodriguez about the latter's family, but it pained Shannon to speak of personal things with the news of his own boy's death still so vivid in his mind. By unspoken consent, they switched to a sporadic discussion of professional matters. After that the two lawmen settled into a companionable silence, concentrating on easing their horses' way over the rough ground and thinking of what might lie ahead of them. After they had been climbing steadily for an hour, Shannon glanced over at Rodriguez's horse.

"How's the sorrel doing?" Shannon asked.

"Excellently, my friend," Rodriguez said. "As I thought, you are a good judge of horseflesh."

"We'll know more about all of these animals when we hit the snow line," Shannon said, looking up at the white expanses far above them.

It was becoming colder now, and the wind blowing along the bare slopes was keen. Soon, however, they entered the seemingly endless forest of fir trees that stretched away above them, and the timber sheltered them from the worst of the gusts. To Shannon's eye the fir trees seemed huge, far larger than the pines that grew in the hills above Whiskey Creek. *Well*, he thought, *at least we won't have any problem finding firewood.*

But every tree might hide a lurking assassin, he reminded himself, and Drago's crew had already proved that they knew how to set up an ambush.

Shannon and Rodriguez had gotten a late start, and in winter darkness came early in the mountains. As the twilight deepened in the forest, the two men turned aside and began to look for shelter for the night. A hundred yards into the woods they found a group of large boulders at the bottom of a knoll. A small stream tumbled down a ravine nearby.

"I guess we'd better bed down here," Shannon said. "If we go on we might stumble into our friend Drago in the dark, and that could be unhealthy."

"*Bueno,*" said Rodriguez, surveying the area. He winked at Shannon. "Ice-cold water to drink and plenty of nice clean stones to lie on. All the comforts of home, no?"

"Well," said Shannon, "anything would be better than that hotel bed in Half Moon City."

They cut some small fir branches to lie on, then unrolled their blankets and wrapped themselves up against the cold. They debated lighting a small fire, but decided not to chance it. A fire would be visible a long way, even in the shelter of the rocks, and the smell of smoke would carry even farther. Water from the stream and a can of beans apiece constituted their dinner. Both water and beans were frigid.

"How much farther do you think it is to the cabin Catlett mentioned?" said Rodriguez, his voice muffled by the blankets.

"I'd say another ten, fifteen miles," Shannon replied.

"We will have to be careful not to come upon it too suddenly," said Rodriguez, yawning.

"Yes," Shannon said absently. He was thinking of Bobby. So much had occurred that morning in Half Moon City that he had not had much time to think of his child's death before this. He had, in fact, deliberately pushed it to the back of his mind so that he could focus on what needed to be done. Now, in the darkness, the painful reality struck him fully for the first time. As he lay there, memories of the past came crowding into his mind. Sundown; the lamps gleaming warmly in the windows of the little house; Kathy setting the table for dinner; Bobby running in to greet him; the boy babbling merrily on as they ate; Kathy smiling happily at both of them as they all sat there together, none of them knowing that it was for the last time.

For Shannon it had been four proud, wonderful years since his son was born. As with so many men who become fathers later in life, Shannon had loved the boy deeply. And now, suddenly, the child was gone forever, killed for no reason by a man without pity, and evil man who had laughed as he threw the little boy from his galloping horse.

And Kathy. What must she have felt as Bobby died? What must she have suffered as she watched the tiny coffin being lowered into the cold ground on Whiskey Creek's windswept Boot Hill? And Shannon had not been there to comfort her. Would she forgive him for not being there? *Get them, Clay*, she had said. *Get them, however long it takes.*

"I'm trying, Kathy," he said, not realizing that he had spoken aloud.

"What did you say, amigo?" said Rodriguez drowsily.

"Nothing," Shannon said. "Sorry."

*I'll get them, Kathy. Somehow, I'll get them. Perhaps tomorrow, perhaps a month from now or a year from now or twenty years from now, but I'll get them.*

He found that he was crying, and was profoundly shocked by the discovery. He had not cried since he was ten years old. Fearful that Rodriguez would become aware of his unmanly tears, he strove to master his emotions. At last, desperately weary in mind and body, he pulled the blankets closer around him and braced himself for the terrible visions that he knew would come to him in the night.

## Chapter Fourteen

They arose before dawn and breakfasted on the remains of the previous evening's beans. The air temperature was near freezing, and the two men moved stiffly about the campsite, trying to restore the circulation to their limbs after a night on the cold ground. They did not make a fire, so there was no coffee to warm them. A long drink of icy water from the stream, and then they were in the saddle again, riding toward whatever the day held in store for them.

They rode very carefully now, watching for telltale tracks. The stony ground told them little. Someone had passed that way not long ago, but it was impossible to say how many or exactly when. As they pushed on, they were constantly looking ahead and to their flanks for any sign that their quarry had left someone behind to watch for them. They had only scant information as to the exact location of the cabin that Catlett had claimed was to be the scene of his reunion with Drago, and thus they had no way of knowing just how close they might be.

Several times they reined in the horses as first Shannon, then Rodriguez dismounted and went ahead on foot through the dense timber to peer cautiously around a bend or over a rise. By noon, the strain was beginning to tell on both of them. Being a potential target for an assassin's bullet hour after hour was hard on the nerves, even for two experienced lawmen. Shannon had tracked men before, many of them, but always in country he knew and with far better odds for his own survival. Now, in this strange new land of towering trees and unknown dangers, he felt an uneasiness that was greater than any he had ever experienced before.

They began to ride past patches of snow lying in the hollows of the ground and the shadows of the trees where the pale sunlight did not reach. Soon, as they moved higher up into the mountains, they found the ground completely covered with snow, and as they rode on the drifts became deeper. The storm that had passed through days before had left its mark. The dark green of the trees stood out in stark contrast to the gray-white of the snowbanks, and several inches of snow now covered the trail. The print of many horses' hooves was plain in the frozen crust. Shannon and Rodriguez pressed forward silently, saying nothing and trying to keep their horses' movements as quiet as they could. This required much of Shannon's attention, for the icy footing was making the buckskin nervous—the animal was not used to snow. Time and the miles dragged by.

Once Shannon looked skyward. Through the thin overcast that was moving in above them, he could see that the sun was now at the zenith. He rubbed his reddened eyes with a gloved hand and shifted uncomfortably in his saddle. Where was the cabin? They should be coming to it soon.

And then the pinto raised its head and whinnied.

Instantly, Shannon was off his horse, wrapping a blanket around the pinto's head to silence him. The wind was blowing down the slope toward them. Had the pinto scented a man or animal that he knew? The crest of a rise lay just ahead, and Shannon could not see what lay beyond it. While he held the pinto quiet, Rodriguez dismounted and moved up the rise, crouched low, rifle in hand. In a moment he was back, his dark eyes glittering with excitement.

"It is just ahead of us," he whispered. "The trail dips down into a little gully and crosses a stream. The cabin is in the woods just beyond."

They tethered the horses and crept through the trees toward the crest. Dropping to their stomachs, they inched their way up to the top and looked over. The stream was a hundred yards below them, the cabin fifty yards beyond that. The rough log structure was just off the path, almost lost in the trees, the snow drifted high along its sides. The tracks they had been following led down the hill, across the stream, and directly to the cabin. The snow in the area in front of the cabin was churned and flattened, as if many riders had paused there, but there were no horses now, and no other sign of life in the vicinity.

"Look," Rodriguez whispered. "The chimney."

Shannon saw that above the little chimney protruding from the cabin's roof, a wisp of smoke hung in the cold air. His muscles tensed as he eased the hammer back on his Winchester, studying the windows, of the cabin for any indication that someone was inside. But the shutters were tightly closed, and there was no way to tell whether the place was still occupied. With no horses in sight, it seemed plausible that whoever had lit the fire in the stove or fireplace beneath that smoking chimney had since moved on, but it was not a possibility that Shannon intended to risk his life upon. Something had caused the pinto to whinny.

They lay there in the snow, watching and listening, for

nearly half an hour. There was no movement outside the cabin, and no indication that anyone was inside. The cabin was quiet, the woods around it apparently empty.

Finally, Shannon motioned to Rodriguez and they backtracked down the rise toward their horses.

"We'll circle around on foot and come up from the rear," Shannon whispered. "Stay behind me and cover me. If anything moves in the woods, count its legs. If it's only got two, shoot it."

Rodriguez nodded his understanding, and they began to work their way through the trees and across the stream to bring them up to the back wall of the cabin. The crust on the snow was fragile, and despite their best efforts it was impossible to move without their boots breaking though. The crunching noise they made sounded as loud as cannon fire to Shannon, but there was no help for it. They had to reach the cabin. Fortunately there were no windows in the back wall of the structure, so that if there were indeed people inside they would not be able to see the lawmen's approach.

After what seemed an eternity, Shannon and Rodriguez found themselves crouched against the rough logs of the blind back wall. They waited there for several minutes, listening intently, Shannon watching the woods to the sides, Rodriguez guarding the rear.

At last a faint sound reached them from inside the cabin. Shannon put his mouth close to Rodriguez's ear.

"Someone's in there, all right," he whispered.

They waited, and the sound came again.

"That is a man groaning in pain," Rodriguez whispered. "I am sure of it."

Shannon nodded in agreement, for he had made the same deduction. They moved as noiselessly as possible around to the side of the cabin, trying to see in through the shuttered window.

"No good," Shannon murmured. "I can't see a thing through the shutter. We'll have to chance the front."

With infinite care they slipped around to the front of the cabin. As they came out of the shelter of the cabin wall, Shannon could feel his skin begin to crawl. They were totally exposed, now. The trail lay just yards away, and anyone hidden in the trees beyond would have an easy shot at them.

"Let's try the door," Shannon whispered. The snow in front of the cabin's entrance was already packed down, so that now their footsteps made little noise. The wooden door was closed. Gingerly, Shannon tried the latch. It moved under his touch.

"Unlocked," Shannon murmured. He looked around again at the trees that surrounded the cabin. "We can't afford to stay out here much longer," he said. "Someone may be drawing a bead on us right now. I think the best bet is to throw open the door and jump inside. When we go through the doorway, I'll hit the floor to the right of the door, you go to the left. If in doubt, shoot. Ready?"

Rodriguez raised his gloved thumb.

"More than ready, amigo," he said. "Out here I feel like one of those sitting ducks you were talking about yesterday."

Shannon reached forward and slowly lifted the latch. It slid silently upward, and the door moved a half-inch inward.

"Now!" Shannon cried. He kicked open the door and dived through, rolling to the right of the doorway and bringing his rifle up to fire at anyone who might be in the cabin. Rodriguez did the same to his left. They lay there, half-winded, their nerves stretched to the breaking point, as they peered around the cabin's darkened interior. There was no one in sight.

They started to rise to their feet.

"Wait a minute," Shannon said. "Look at that bunk over there. Someone's lying under those blankets." He stepped swiftly across the rough wooden floor and jammed the muzzle of his rifle into the mound of blankets on the bunk. The result was another groan, followed by a series of coughs. Shannon flipped back the blankets with his left hand, the index finger of his right hand tight on the trigger of the rifle. A bearded man lay doubled up on the bunk. He was clad only in faded woolen long underwear and his eyes were closed. The woolen fabric was soaked in blood.

"Do you recognize him?" Rodriguez asked, peering at the motionless man in the dim light.

"No," said Shannon, "but I'm pretty sure he wasn't among the men who were at Whiskey Creek. If he's one of Drago's boys, he's one I haven't seen before."

He looked around the cramped cabin. The fire on the hearth was nearly out, but the glowing embers gave enough light to reveal the contours of the room. Against one wall lay a jumble of small steel traps, and nearby a single ragged beaver pelt was crumpled on the floor.

"Trapper," said Shannon. "Using the cabin for shelter on his way down to the lowlands, I guess. Drago and his men must have found him here and shot him."

Rodriguez kicked at the pile of traps.

"I do not like trappers," he said. "The animals they catch in these traps suffer greatly. I have no sympathy and no respect for anyone who would earn his living by such cruelty."

"Well," Shannon said, kneeling beside the bunk, "it looks like the trapper's the one doing the suffering now. Bullet wound in his side and another in his leg. It's a wonder he hasn't bled to death." He shook the wounded man roughly, trying to rouse him. The man groaned again and opened his eyes. When he saw Shannon close beside him his face blanched in sheer terror.

"Don't shoot me again!" he cried. "Please don't shoot me again!"

"We're not going to hurt you, mister," Shannon said. "We're lawmen. Who are you?"

"Name's McBride," the man wheezed, trying to focus his eyes on Shannon. "Colorado Jack, they call me. Help me, will ya? I'm hurt bad."

"Who shot you?" said Rodriguez.

"Dunno. Some men busted in here a while ago. They plugged me and threw me on the bunk here, laughin' like loons. I passed out for a spell, and when I came to they wuz gone. Took my food and my rifle and my pelts, blast 'em. Left my shotgun, though, by thunder. There it is, on the floor over there by the door." McBride waved weakly in that direction, then slumped back. "Glad I still got my shotgun," he mumbled. His eyes were glazed and unfocused, but he was still talking, though his speech was slurred. "Got an Injun with it one night over on the Yellowstone river," he mumbled. "The ornery cuss tried to sneak up on me in the dark, and I—"

"Tell us about your glorious deeds later, McBride," Shannon said impatiently. "The men who shot you—how long ago did they leave?"

"Can't say. Like I said, they wuz gone when I came around. Say, can't you do nothin' to stop this bleedin'? I tried, but I ain't got the strength."

Shannon searched the cabin until he found an old shirt on a shelf on the wall. He ripped the shirt into strips and bound up McBride's wounds as best he could. The man moaned piteously as Shannon tightened the bandages. Then the trapper closed his eyes again and lay back, muttering incoherently to himself.

Shannon and Rodriguez moved to the other side of the cabin and spoke in low tones so that the half-conscious McBride would not overhear.

"The gang can't have been gone very long," Shannon said. "That fire is only just now dying out, and it's a cinch McBride didn't put any more wood on it after he was shot. Our friends may be only an hour or so ahead of us."

"Then let us hurry," said Rodriguez. "With a little good fortune, we can catch up to them before dark."

Shannon shook his head.

"We've got a problem," he said. "That man on the bunk needs a doctor. He's badly hurt."

"He is nearly dead right now," said Rodriguez. "If we move him, he will probably die anyway. Is it worth what it will cost us to help him?" He and Shannon looked at each other, sharing the same thought. The men they were hunting were at most a few miles ahead, almost within reach. If the lawmen turned back now to take the wounded trapper to safety, they would lose at least two days' time. The outlaws would be far away by then, and the effort to save McBride might be in vain anyway, for, as Rodriguez had suggested, hauling the injured trapper back down the rocky hillsides could well kill him long before they reached Half Moon City. Shannon ached with every fiber of his being to mount up and go after the bandits, but once again duty barred his path.

"We can't just leave him here," Shannon said reluctantly. "It wouldn't be right."

And that was the dilemma. If they left the wounded trapper to die, they would be no better than the men they were chasing.

Rodriguez raised his hands in resignation. "You are right, amigo," he said. "It is bad luck, but we must do what must be done. Yes, we will assist this animal-killer regardless of the consequences."

He paused for a moment, analyzing the situation. Shannon waited. A plan was forming in his mind, but he wanted Rodriguez to think of it first.

"I suppose," Rodriguez said, "we could make a travois, Indian-style, and get him back down to Half Moon City that way."

"Yes," Shannon said. "And it would only take one of us to do that."

"But which of us will go?" asked Rodriguez. He looked unhappy, as if he already knew the answer.

"I've seen Drago and his men," Shannon said. "I'd know them if I saw them again. You wouldn't. Looks like you're elected good Samaritan."

"It is the logical thing, I suppose," Rodriguez said disconsolately.

"I'll bring up the horses," said Shannon, "and then we'll cut some big branches to make the travois. We can use the blankets from the bunk to cover it. While I'm rounding up the livestock, can you stoke up that fire a little?"

"I will see to it," said Rodriguez. He went to the pile of wood that lay against the wall near the hearth and tossed several pieces onto the dying fire.

Shannon propped his rifle in a corner and opened the door. It was very nearly his last act on earth.

## Chapter Fifteen

As Shannon stepped through the cabin doorway, the sharp crack of a rifle echoed through the forest, and a bullet buried itself in the doorframe inches from his head. Shannon just had time enough to see the smoke blossom in the trees across the trail before he was back inside the cabin, slamming the door behind him and flattening himself against the wall.

"Looks like we've got company," he said, picking up the Winchester and edging toward the shuttered window. "Whoever fired at me must be a fool. If he'd waited until I'd taken a few more steps he'd have had me cold."

Rodriguez went to the other window and peered through a small chink in the shutter.

"One of them is back in the woods a few yards," Shannon said. "I saw the smoke when he fired." He removed the bar on the shutter and eased the panel open slowly, trying to see into the shadows where the enemy was hiding. Another shot echoed from the trees, and this time the bullet drilled a neat hole in the shutter, narrowly missing Shannon's head and striking the opposite wall of the cabin.

Shannon crouched down again behind the shelter of the log walls, striving to think clearly. Their position was not a good one. There was only the one door, and that was in front, in full view of the unknown riflemen. The two front windows would likewise be under fire. There was a window in each side of the cabin, but anyone trying to slip out that way would be seen easily from the woods beyond the trail, and if there were more than one or two gunmen, both sides of the cabin would surely be covered by the others anyway. Shannon and Rodriguez were neatly trapped.

Rodriguez was still peering through the crack in the shutter on his side of the door.

"See anyone?" Shannon asked.

"No. Whoever it is, they're well hidden."

Shannon cautiously raised himself up to take a look. Another bullet knocked splinters from the windowsill beside his ear.

Shannon raised his rifle and fired twice in the general direction of the powder smoke drifting among the trees.

"Do you see them?" Rodriguez asked.

"No," said Shannon, again ducking down behind the safety of the wall. "I just wanted to let them know we're still dangerous."

He raised up and snapped another shot into the trees. This time several shots were fired in return, the slugs slamming into the windowsill and perforating the shutter.

"There's at least two of them," Shannon said, crouching down again.

"Unfortunately, two may be enough," Rodriguez said disgustedly. "You and I should be ashamed for letting ourselves be caught like this. We must be getting careless in our old age."

"Spilled milk, my friend," said Shannon. He was looking

around the cabin, searching for a solution. To go out through the door or the windows was certain death. To remain inside was little better, for their tormentors would then have several courses of action open to them. It was now late afternoon, and if a significant number of men were out there, at nightfall they could rush the cabin and over-whelm Shannon and Rodriguez. Or they could choose to keep the two lawmen penned inside the cabin indefinitely. Their supplies were still on their horses tethered beyond the rise, well hidden but far beyond reach. And there was, so far as Shannon could see, neither food nor water inside the cabin. A patient adversary could literally starve them out. But did the people across the trees have the time for that? Unlikely. No, they would make a move soon, perhaps as soon as darkness fell. He had to anticipate their plan, put himself in their place and predict their actions.

As he pondered the situation, he could not convince him-self that just two men had sprung the trap. There had to be at least three or four, possibly more than that. Yet only one or two men seemed to be firing, and they were shooting at the front of the cabin. Why?

The fire on the hearth was burning brightly now, and Shannon examined the room more carefully. There were several shelves on one wall, but since Shannon had re-moved the old shirt from one of them to bandage McBride, they were bare. A crude table sat at one side of the room. It, too, was bare. Beside the table was a single chair, now lying on its side. In a corner near the pile of firewood stood a rusty axe, used to cut the firewood, no doubt. There were also four oil lamps, one hanging on each wall, none of them lit. Two bunks were built against the back wall; McBride occupied one of them, and the other was empty, without a mattress or even a blanket on it. Beyond that, the room was empty.

But a still, small voice in his head was nagging at Shannon as he completed his inventory. There was something missing. Something that should be there, but wasn't.

"Pete," he said, keeping his voice level, "do you see any coal oil anywhere in here?"

"No," said Rodriguez. "Why?"

"There are four oil lamps," said Shannon. "Why isn't there any oil for them?"

"What does it matter?" said Rodriguez, puzzled. "Perhaps it has just been used up. Besides, we will not be using lamps if we are still in here tonight. To show a light would be dangerous, and it would ruin our night vision as well."

"Still," said Shannon, "it seems curious . . ."

And then he realized what was going to happen.

"You were right, Pete," he said. "We truly have made fools of ourselves. This isn't just another drygulching. Those people must have heard what happened to the last bushwhackers they left in the trees to ambush a posse, and they didn't want to take us on head to head. No, a very special trap has been set for us, and we've obligingly walked into it, like lambs to the slaughter."

"What do you mean?"

"Those people must have been out there waiting for us when we came bumbling up here like a pair of tenderfooted tourists. They could have opened fire on us anytime. But instead they waited until we were inside. Why?"

Rodriguez laughed. "The *banditos* must think very highly of us, *compadre*," he said. "It seems they do not want to chance an open fight with us, even when they have all the advantages. I suppose we should be flattered that we strike such fear into their hearts. But what is this sinister plan you speak of?"

"Remember when I started out the door and I said they were foolish to fire too soon? Well, it wasn't foolishness— they want to keep us in here."

"So the rest can get away?"

"That could be part of it, but I think they want more than that. There's hatred out there in those trees, Pete. I can feel it. Drago himself may or may not be out there, but it's his plan, I'll bet anything on it. It's just the sort of thing he'd do."

"But why would they go to so much trouble? As you said, if they just want to kill us, they could have easily shot us when we were approaching the cabin."

"They want more than our deaths," Shannon said. "They want revenge. Revenge against me, I guess—revenge for Catlett, revenge for the men I've shot in the past few days, revenge for their friends and relatives I killed six years ago when we were cleaning up Whiskey Creek. They don't just want to kill us, they want to do it in the nastiest possible way."

"The missing coal oil!" exclaimed Rodriguez. "They have it!"

"Yes, and this shack has a blind side, the same side we came up on. If I'm right, they'll sneak up that way, soak the wall and the roof with coal oil, and light it. We won't be able to stop them because we can't see them coming from that direction. And when the fire starts, they've got the door and the windows covered. These old logs and that flimsy roof will burn like paper, and within minutes you and I will have a tough choice to make—stay in here and fry, or go out there knowing we're going to be shot full of holes when we do."

He shook his head in grudging admiration.

"It's a good plan, too. We'll be right under their guns whether we go out the door or the windows, and it won't matter if it's dark by then because the whole place will be lit up like a New Year's bonfire."

"If you are right, they will be coming for us soon," Rodriguez said, risking a quick look through the crack in the shutter of the front window. "It is getting dark now." He looked again at Shannon, his jaw firmly set. "Amigo," he said, "I do not wish to stay in here like a trapped rat, waiting to burn to death. When the time comes, let us go out that door together and fight them. Maybe we will be lucky."

"Maybe we won't," said Shannon, "but at least we'll take a few of them with us."

"We are not dead yet, my friend," Rodriguez said. "We have been in tight places before, you and I."

"True," said Shannon with a rueful smile, "but this is the tightest one I can remember. If we don't get out of this, I hope you'll forgive me for getting you killed."

Rodriguez chuckled. "Many men have tried to kill me," he said, "but so far no one has succeeded. Perhaps you will fail also, eh?"

There was a sudden scuffling sound on the other side of the back wall, and they could hear liquid splashing across the wall and onto the low roof.

"When the fire starts," Shannon said, "we'll wait as long as we can. By that time the smoke will be thick enough to make it hard for them to see. Then we'll go out the windows, you on that side, and I on this one. That will divide their fire."

"What about this McBride?" Rodriguez said. "I would not want to leave any man to burn."

"He'll have to take his chances, too. Even if he recovers consciousness in time, he won't be able to walk, and if we dump him out a window ahead of us they'll just shoot him first. I think the best bet is to lay him on the floor near the front door and leave the door unlocked. Maybe he can crawl out while they're busy with us. Or if one of us survives, we can reach through the door and drag him outside, hopefully before the roof collapses on him."

"A long chance, amigo. For all of us."

"Better suggestions will be cheerfully accepted," Shannon said. He noted with surprise that he was actually grinning. Instead of fear, he felt a curious sort of euphoria. Incredibly, insanely, he found himself excited, almost happy, at the prospect of a fight. Indeed, he could hardly wait for the moment when he would be going out the window, through the flames, and into the muzzles of the outlaws' guns. It was as if the danger, the deadly danger, was acting as some sort of intoxicant upon him. Or was it just that, grieving for his dead child, he wanted to die himself, and was eager for the moment?

The clank of metal sounded outside the rear wall.

"They've thrown down the coal oil can," Shannon said. "Now they'll light the fire."

Almost immediately they heard the rush of flame as the oil-soaked logs ignited. Smoke began to pour through the chinks in the logs of the back wall, and within seconds the fire was eating through the tinder-dry wooden shingles of the roof. The roar of the flames filled the room, nearly deafening them.

"Get the bars off all the shutters," Shannon called to Rodriguez, "and then help me move McBride over by the door." He went to the bunk and hauled the semiconscious trapper into a sitting position. The man moaned piteously and opened his eyes, peering around him with a dazed expression.

"McBride!" said Shannon, taking him by the shoulders, "McBride, can you hear me?"

"What's happening?" McBride grunted. "What's that smoke?" His face was gray and he was sweating profusely in the cold air of the cabin.

"The men who shot you have set the cabin on fire," Shannon bellowed in McBride's ear. "We're going to get you out if we can. Right now we're going to carry you over to the door. It's going to hurt, but we can't help that. I'll leave the door ajar for you. Lie there until the roof starts to cave in, then push the door open and crawl out. One of us will come back to help you if we can, but if we can't you'll have to save yourself. Do you understand?"

"Yeah," the trapper said. He was alert now as fright drove the cobwebs from his mind. "The ones out there, they're the people who shot me."

"Yes," said Shannon. "They're after us, too. We're going to try to get them before they get us."

Smoke now filled the cabin. A burning ceiling beam came crashing down around them, scattering sparks across the floor. Little fires sprang up where the sparks landed. Shannon and Rodriguez dragged McBride to the front of the cabin and left him by the door. Another piece of burning wood fell, searing Shannon's neck before glancing off his shoulder.

"Time to go," he said to Rodriguez.

"*Vaya con Dios*, amigo."

"*Vaya con Dios*, Pedro. Thanks for everything."

Silently they shook hands.

"Do not worry, my friend," said Rodriguez, checking the cylinder of his revolver. "We will find our way out of this. I am certain of it."

"Let's get to the windows," Shannon said, coughing in the smoke. "I'll give the word and we'll both go out at the same time."

The roof was now fully ablaze, and fire was licking through the chinks in the logs and racing up the inside walls. A large flaming beam came down, narrowly missing Rodriguez. Shannon drew his Colt.

"*Now!*" he cried.

In perfect unison, Shannon and Rodriguez yanked open the shutters of their respective side windows, tossed their Winchester rifles out the openings, and dived through after them.

Shannon landed on his head in a snowbank beside the wall. Gunfire erupted in the woods. The dense smoke pouring out of the burning cabin obscured the gun flashes, making them seem distant and unreal. Shannon scooped the Winchester out of the snow with his left hand and dashed for the front of the cabin, holding his six-gun ready as he ran. Bullets were kicking up the snow all around him and gouging chunks out of the log walls as he passed. From the other side of the building he could hear more gunshots, and he knew that Rodriguez must be under fire also. Indeed, for all Shannon knew, at that very moment Rodriguez might already be lying dead in the snow.

Yet Shannon lived. As he ran along the wall, his face and hands were stung by splinters kicked up by the bullet strikes on the logs. He felt a searing pain across the small of his back, and something tugged sharply at the heel of his right boot. As he reached the corner of the cabin, the silhouette of a man materialized through the smoke, backlighted by the flames reflecting on the packed snow. The shadow fired at Shannon, but the bullet went wide. Shannon put two quick shots into the silhouette, and it tumbled to the ground. Shannon jumped over it and rounded the corner. Two more men were standing in front of the cabin door, their rifles pointed at the doorway. When they saw Shannon they pivoted to fire at him. Shannon thumbed the hammer of the Colt twice more. One of the men went down, but the other was still there, raising his rifle. Pedro Rodriguez came around the other side of the cabin, saw what was happening, and shot the man in the back. Shannon put another .45 slug in him as he went down.

Shannon glanced quickly at Rodriguez and saw that there was blood running down his left arm. Then another ghostly form was running at them through the smoke, firing at them, and Rodriguez fell heavily to the ground. Shannon pulled the trigger of his six-gun again, but the hammer dropped on an empty chamber. The oncoming gunman raised his rifle. Only then did Shannon realize that it was

Cooper, the ex-marshal of Half Moon City. Cooper bawled, "This is for you, Shannon! Right in the belly!" Then, abruptly, Cooper fell dead on the ground, blasted by a shotgun fired from the open front door of the cabin. McBride came crawling out, dragging his shotgun with him. He collapsed in the snow in front of the door, the firelight dancing wildly over his prostrate figure.

"Gotcha, you sidewinder," McBride gasped. "I'll teach you to shoot me, you . . ."

Shannon had now holstered his revolver and was holding the cocked Winchester at the ready, swiveling back and forth as he swept his field of view for more enemies. Two men were staggering away from the cabin toward the woods. Shannon fired, and one of them went down. The other man caught the fallen one by the collar and pulled him into the treeline. Somewhere in the trees, horses were moving, their hoofbeats just audible above the crackle of the fire that had now all but consumed the cabin.

A voice came echoing out of the forest as the unseen horses broke into a gallop.

"Next time, Shannon," the voice cried. "Next time for sure!" Several horsemen came charging out of the trees and fled away up the trail. As the last man passed through the far edge of the firelight, Shannon saw that it was Drago.

The bile rose in Shannon's throat. This was the man who had butchered his son and broken his wife's heart, the man who had repeatedly tried to kill him, and who now, perhaps, had killed his best friend. He threw the rifle to his shoulder and fired repeatedly at the retreating outlaw, jacking shell after shell into the chamber until the rifle clicked empty. But the light was bad and the range too great, and the momentary glimpse Shannon had obtained through the smoke was not enough to give his stinging eyes and shaking hands a chance to do their work. Drago disappeared into the darkness, hurling obscenities back over his shoulder. Shannon dropped the rifle and stood there with clenched fists, staring. He had no means of pursuing Drago and his weapons were now useless. Every muscle in Shannon's body trembled with anger and frustration as he watched his enemy fade safely away into the night.

"You made one mistake, Drago," Shannon shouted hoarsely after the departing outlaw. "You didn't kill me! I'm still alive! And I'm coming for you, Drago! No matter where you hide, I'm coming for you!"

Then Shannon's legs gave way beneath him, and he fell to his knees on the blood-spattered, firelit snow, emotionally drained and physically exhausted.

## Chapter Sixteen

As his head began to clear, Shannon looked around him. The glare of the burning cabin bathed the snow and the nearby trees in its flickering, eerie light. The cabin itself was now totally engulfed in flames, and the air was filled with their hissing and crackling. The leaping fire sent clouds of sparks soaring upward into the black, starless sky. The roof of the cabin and one of the walls had caved in. Even as Shannon watched, two more collapsed, scattering burning embers across the snow and sending more angry sparks billowing high into the night. In front of the cabin, Shannon could see two bodies sprawled facedown in the snow. The dancing light of the fire made the corpses appear to shudder and writhe, but it was only an illusion, for the men were quite dead. They lay as they had fallen, their limbs tangled grotesquely.

Still half-dazed, Shannon suddenly remembered that he had seen Pedro Rodriguez fall to the ground during the gunfight. Fear gripped him. Was one of these two dead men his friend? He limped through the snow to them and rolled each one over, then breathed a sigh of relief. Both of the corpses were Drago's men.

But where was Rodriguez?

"Pedro!" he called. "Pete!"

"Over here, amigo," Rodriguez replied. He was sitting on the icy ground a few yards behind Shannon. His face and clothes were covered with soot, and he was attempting to tie a bandanna around his wounded arm.

"How bad is it?" Shannon said, kneeling beside him.

"A scratch only," said Rodriguez indifferently. "I have cut myself more seriously when shaving. The worst part is that those accursed *banditos* have put a hole in the sleeve of the fine new coat you bought for me in Half Moon City."

"I saw you go down," Shannon said. "I thought they'd killed you."

"Ah, that. I am embarrassed to say that I merely slipped on the ice. The only injury was to my dignity. And you, my friend? How are you?"

Until then, Shannon had forgotten about his own condition. Now, as the flow of adrenaline slowed and rational thought returned, he began to feel the effects of the evening's events. His neck was burned where the blazing board had fallen against it, and his back where the bullet had creased him felt as if someone had laid a whip across it.

"Singed a bit, and a little skin missing," Shannon said. "Nothing important. Two of the gunmen are over there, dead, and I know we wounded at least two or three more before they ran. We were lucky, my friend. We escaped their trap, and we're still alive. Miracles do happen, I guess."

"Yes, we were lucky," Rodriguez said with a grin, "but we were also good. We outfought them, amigo, you and I. They had us cold, and we outfought them. They will think carefully before attacking us again."

He looked over at the corpse of ex-Marshal Cooper.

"Is that the one McBride got with the shotgun?" he said, crossing himself.

"Yes," said Shannon. "It's our pal Cooper, or at least it was. Looks like he decided to throw in with Drago, just as we thought he might. Probably helped Drago plan this little party for us."

"Well," said Rodriguez, "it was a very brief partnership."

Shannon realized for the first time that the two of them were still in the open, silhouetted against the firelight.

"If we don't get out of this glare," he said, "we may be dead ourselves. Let's get into the trees and wait a bit to make sure all of them have gone. Then we can congratulate ourselves and toast a marshmallow or two."

"Hey, you fellers," a hoarse voice called feebly from the ground a few feet away. "What about me?"

It was the wounded trapper, McBride. He was lying where he had fallen just outside the cabin, his shotgun still clutched in his hand.

"We'd better move him before that last wall falls on him," Shannon said. "Give me a hand, will you?"

They dragged the trapper away from the burning cabin. He cried out several times as they pulled him into the shadows of the trees.

"Nice work with that shotgun back there, McBride," Shannon said. But the old trapper had fainted again and did not hear him.

"What next?" Rodriguez asked.

"First we'd better see if we still have any horses," Shannon said. "If the outlaws found them and took them, we'll be in trouble. Stay with McBride while I have a look."

Trying to ignore the pain where the bullet had furrowed the flesh of his back, Shannon crossed the stream and climbed the rise, reloading his weapons as he went. Once he was out of the light of the burning cabin, the forest and the night made it difficult for him to get his bearings. He moved cautiously from tree to tree, half expecting a bullet from some watcher in the woods.

A moment later he breathed a sigh of relief. Their horses were still tethered in the hollow where they had been left. Due to good fortune or the care with which Shannon and Rodriguez had concealed the animals, the outlaws had not found them.

Shannon led the three horses back to the edge of the woods where Rodriguez and McBride awaited him. They wrapped McBride in their spare blankets and gave him some water. The trapper thanked them feebly and closed his eyes.

"We've got to get him down to the valley where he can get some help," Shannon said. "It's amazing that he's still alive. Let's see if our late guests left any horseflesh behind that might do to pull the travois. No use using your horse or the pack horse for that unless we have to."

Cautiously, they slipped into the trees where the outlaws had hidden. As they entered the tree line they heard noises ahead of them, and a moment later there was movement in the underbrush. Both men crouched down, ready to shoot, but all that came out of the shadows was a thin gray horse with a frightened expression, dragging its broken reins along the ground.

"Marshal Cooper's gray gelding, I'll wager," said Shannon. "Looks like our dear departed friend left us a little inheritance." He caught the reins and calmed the animal. "You can use him to help you get McBride back down the mountain," he said. "Now let's see if there are any other horses roaming around. Should be a couple of them that were formerly owned by the gents on the ground back there."

They searched for some minutes, but found no more loose animals.

"The survivors led them away, most likely," Shannon said, disappointed. "I'd like to have had a look at their saddlebags. We haven't yet seen any of the cash that was stolen from the bank in Whiskey Creek, and I want to recover at least some of it if I can."

"A few of the *banditos* must have ridden on ahead while the others set their trap for us," said Rodriguez. "It may be that the ones who moved on had the bank loot with them."

"You're probably right," said Shannon. "But I'm surprised that Drago was willing to let any of it out of his sight. I wouldn't expect trust to be one of his virtues—if he has any. I'll bet his share is still tucked neatly behind his own saddle."

They took one last look around.

"It's no use," Shannon said. "If any more horses are out here, we'll never find them in the dark. Come on, let's get moving. Time is against us now."

Shannon took some of the supplies from the pack horse and gave them to Rodriguez. Then, working swiftly, they constructed a travois from some large branches cut from the nearby trees, stretching blankets over the frame to make a place for McBride. They lifted the half-conscious man into the contraption and tied it behind the gray horse they had found in the woods. The animal shied at first, unaccustomed to having something dragging behind it, but it soon calmed down and stood quietly. Rodriguez gathered up the lead line and the reins of his own horse and prepared to start his errand of mercy.

"So," said Rodriguez, "what will you be doing while I am rescuing the redoubtable Señor McBride?"

"I'm going after Drago. The tracks in the snow should be fresh and plain, so I may be able to do it even in the dark."

"If you catch up to them, you will be badly outnumbered. Surely it would be safer to wait until daylight."

"Safer, yes. But they're so close now, Pete. So very close. I don't want them to get another big lead on us. As for being outnumbered, well, I've been outnumbered before."

He took a stick and drew a rough map in the snow.

"Here we are now," he said. "The trail climbs over this mountain range and then another. After you've delivered McBride, you can come after me. I'll leave plenty of sign for you to follow."

"And if you lose them?"

Shannon considered the alternatives.

"If I can't follow their tracks, or you can't follow mine, we'll meet in three days at the Wind River Indian Agency. According to my information, it's right . . . here." He drew an "x" on the map in the snow. "If I get there first, and they're not there, I'll wait for you. If you get there first, you wait for me. If I don't catch them, I'll come there."

"And if you do not come?" said Rodriguez. "How long should I wait?"

"If I'm not there within the week," Shannon said, "I'm not coming at all, and you can head back for Dry Wells."

Rodriguez scowled.

"I do not like letting you go on alone," he said. "Señora Shannon will be angry with me. And if you get yourself killed before I can rejoin you, I will be angry with *you*. Besides, I will miss all the fun."

"I'll be careful," Shannon said. "And if I find them, I'll save some for you."

Shannon waited until Rodriguez and his moaning burden were out of sight, then took the lead line of the pack horse, mounted the buckskin, and started out again. Once he had passed beyond the light from the dying fire, the forest and the night enfolded him. The sky was overcast, so there was no moonlight or even starlight to guide him. Only the faint sheen of the snow on the ground enabled him to follow the tracks, and it was slow going, for he had to dismount periodically to study the ground to be sure that the fleeing horsemen had not left the beaten path and vanished into the forest.

Despite the difficulties, the tracks were sufficiently clear to enable him to follow them for several hours. The temperature was dropping, and even in the near-total darkness Shannon could see his breath in the cold air as he groped his way along. He had now been without food for a day and a night and he was ravenously hungry, but he vowed to himself that whatever else happened, he would never stop to eat or rest as long as he could make out the hoofprints of the bandits's horses ahead of him.

In the hour before the dawn, it began to snow. Shannon urged the buckskin forward, trying to keep the tracks in sight, but soon the snow was falling more heavily, and within half an hour it had covered all traces of the outlaws' passage. Now Shannon had no way of knowing if the men he was hunting had continued straight ahead or turned off somewhere into the forest. Each time he came upon a stream coursing down the mountain, he had to dismount and try to determine whether the horsemen might have gone upstream or downstream to cover their escape. But in the darkness it was impossible to tell, and soon he had to admit to himself that he was only guessing. Still he rode doggedly on, his instinct whispering to him that Drago and his cohorts would stay on the trail and not strike off cross-country. Once off the beaten track, they would have found it very difficult to move through the dark woods and the deepening snow, and in any event they must have some goal in mind, some destination, and that was much more likely to lie on the trail than off it.

After a night that seemed to last forever, the sky began at last to lighten, but the gray dawn provided him with little help. The tracks of the horses he was following were no longer visible, even in the daylight. The new snowfall had defeated him. All he could do was push on, hoping for some sign to indicate that he was still on the right course.

There was no sunrise because of the scudding clouds that obscured the sky, and two hours after dawn the light was still gray and the snow unrevealing. The buckskin was showing signs of weariness, and several times Shannon found himself dozing as the horse plodded along. Once Shannon fell completely asleep for a few seconds, nearly falling out of the saddle. Clearly this was not a safe method of tracking men who might at any time double back and wait for an opportunity to kill him. Furthermore, Shannon knew that both he and his animals were nearing the limits of endurance. His main concern was for the horses. It would not do to have them foundering here in the wilds, leaving him afoot. Shannon was nothing if not a realist, and the realities of the present situation could no longer be ignored. Cursing the frailties of man and beast, he unwillingly left the trail and rode into a small hollow where the boulders had prevented the snow from drifting too deeply.

Shannon fed the horses from the dwindling supply of grain, for there was nothing upon which they could graze in the snow. He was tempted to make a fire and heat some coffee, but decided against it. Instead he drank the cold water from his canteen and opened another can of beans. They were congealed and tasteless, but he knew he needed food, however cold and unpalatable, to give him strength to go on.

He let the horses rest for a time while he unrolled his blankets and sat against a tree. Despite his efforts to stay awake, the weariness overcame him, and presently he found himself dozing off. Annoyed by his own weakness, he rolled up the blankets, remounted, and resumed the chase, urging the tired horses along and trying to stay alert.

It was fortunate that he did so, for scarcely a mile farther along he noticed an odd-shaped lump lying just a few feet off the trail, thinly covered with new snow. Shannon was nearly past it when it registered on him, and he reined in the buckskin abruptly. The weary pack horse was slow to react and bumped into the buckskin. Both horses snorted in protest. Shannon soothed them, then dismounted and walked over to the irregular shape in the snow. Even before he reached it, he knew what it was. He began to brush away the coverlet of white that obscured the object, and almost immediately found himself staring at a human eye gazing blankly up at him through its icy shroud. In a few more moments he had uncovered the corpse sufficiently to see that it was bloody and already stiff. A bullet hole low in the back told its story—it was one of the outlaws who had been wounded in the fight at the cabin. In fact, it appeared to be the man whom Shannon had shot in front of the cabin, the man who had been dragged into the woods by one of the other gang members before Shannon could bring them down permanently. The wounded man had apparently ridden this far before succumbing. His companions, not wishing to be encumbered with a corpse, had simply tossed him into the snowdrift and left him there.

It had been a rash as well as a callous thing to do. By leaving the body right beside the trail, the outlaws had told Shannon what he most wanted to know—that he was still on their trail, that they were still somewhere up ahead of him. Looking at the corpse, Shannon felt a moment's regret that circumstances had reduced him to killing men by shooting them in the back. However, he decided that, considering the situation at the time, he could still live with himself. He searched the man's pockets, but found only a plug of tobacco and a rusty jackknife. There was nothing on the dead man's person to identify him or give Shannon any indication as to where he might have been headed. Nor was there any money. But the vital clue was there—he was still on the right track. Now he had some incentive to press on into the snowstorm despite his hunger and fatigue.

Shannon rolled the dead man over and left him where his friends had discarded him. *One more, Kathy*, he said to the sky. *One more of the men who killed our child. Soon, tomorrow perhaps, I'll find the rest.*

Shannon remounted the buckskin and rode on, still fighting to stay awake in the saddle and to watch for trouble along the way. The wind was picking up, blowing down the mountainside directly into the faces of Shannon and his animals. Shannon muffled himself in his coat, pulled his hat down low over his eyes, and urged the nearly spent horses on and on, hour after hour.

But even the most driven of men has his limits, and by late afternoon Shannon had reached his. The horses too were nearly done, and although Shannon had no sympathy with his own human failings, he at last took pity on the worn-out beasts.

Although it was scarcely 4:00, the woods were already receding into twilight. He must find a place to shelter, for night would soon be falling, and even if he had been able to do so he did not want to risk pressing on in the dark again. He had already pushed his luck too far in that respect. He must abandon the chase until the morning brought enough daylight to see by.

He looked around, hoping for another cluster of big boulders or at least a particularly thick stand of trees where he could find some protection from the elements. Within moments he saw, just a few yards into the woods, a cliff overhanging a shallow cave. The cave was not large, but it was protected from the storm by a rocky ledge that protruded out several feet from the cliff side, and the snow had not yet drifted into it. Knowing it was the best he could do, Shannon guided the horses into the shelter of the overhang.

Tethering the buckskin and the pinto, he made his modest camp. The horses were fed another generous helping from the supply of grain that remained on the packhorse, for there was still nothing upon which the hungry animals could graze. As the buckskin munched contentedly, Shannon stroked the silky neck.

"Thanks, partner," he said softly. "I wish I didn't have to push you so hard, but we've got a score to settle. Plenty of time to rest later."

Once the horses had been attended to, Shannon unrolled his blankets and began to prepare himself a much-needed meal. After some thought he decided to chance a small fire, for he desperately wanted some hot food and some hot coffee. *The fire's a dangerous luxury*, he reminded himself. *In the darkness, it will be visible a long way. Is a cup of hot coffee worth dying for?* Upon reflection, he decided that in this case it probably was. Soon the coffee was boiling, and he drank it without waiting for it to cool. The scalding, bitter liquid tasted to Shannon like the nectar of the gods.

The snow had finally stopped, and the wind had died away. Shannon cooked some bacon to go with the coffee, hoping that the odor of the frying meat would not attract the attention of any wild animals, four-footed or otherwise.

As he ate and drank he watched night fall in the forest. He looked up beyond the dark trees and saw that the clouds that had brought the snow were thinning. With the disappearance of the cloud cover it was growing colder, and he pulled the blankets close around him as he ate. Here and there a star began to twinkle in the blackness above him, and once a meteorite flashed across the sky and was gone.

Shannon watched the deepening night, feeling the solitude around him and wondering what the next day had in store. He had been forced to stop and rest, and so might have lost ground in his deadly chase. But then the outlaws would have to rest sometime, too. Whatever time he lost now would be nullified by their stopping for the night as well. If they did stop. Would they? Yes, surely they must. It was unlikely that they would realize how closely he was pursuing them. And in any event, it didn't matter whether they stopped or not. He would find them. He would. Sometime.

Finishing his meager repast, Shannon put out the tiny fire and checked the horses one more time. Then he wrapped himself up in his blankets and contemplated the stars until his eyelids closed.

## Chapter Seventeen

Shannon had no more than dozed off when the buckskin began to snort and paw the ground, warning that it had heard or scented something. Shannon slipped out of his blankets and crouched under the ledge, listening. With the wind gone and the forest now still, he knew that even small noises would carry a great distance in the cold air. He eased a cartridge into the chamber of the Winchester and waited.

At last he heard the sound he had been expecting. A horseman was coming up the trail in the same direction he had been traveling. The hoofbeats were muffled by the snow, but they were unmistakable. Rodriguez? No, it was far too soon for him to have completed his errand of mercy with the injured trapper and returned. Who then? A chance traveler? But who would travel this lonely path in the dark? Perhaps one of the outlaws had gotten behind him and was now tracking him, hoping for a shot at his back. Well, he would soon know.

There was a slight bend in the trail just below him, and

the forest obscured the oncoming horseman until he was quite near. Then Shannon's straining eyes, aided by the starlight and the snow, saw the dark shape of the horse and rider coming out from among the trees. The man was moving slowly, head down, but he did not appear to be tracking anyone. Rather, he seemed just to be coming doggedly on, oblivious to his surroundings, riding through the darkness toward some unknown destination. His hat was pulled down over his forehead, and in the faint light his features could not be seen.

Shannon had two choices: He could remain hidden and let the rider pass by, but that would mean that some unknown individual would be out there ahead of him. Or he could challenge the solitary horseman, stop him, and discover his identity and his purpose. Either way there was danger, but in the end curiosity won out. Shannon moved noiselessly down to a large fir tree near the edge of the trail and held the rifle at the ready. As the horseman drew even with him, he stepped out from behind the tree and drew a bead on the rider's shadowy form.

"Hold it, mister," Shannon barked. "Rein up and then keep your hands high and still. I've got a rifle on you, and if you make me nervous I'll use it."

"C-Clay?" said a small voice. "Clay, is that you?"

Shannon was so surprised that he almost dropped the rifle.

"Kathy!" he said. "What in heaven's name—"

Kathy Shannon jumped down from the horse and ran to him. Even in the darkness it was apparent that she was weeping with relief.

"Oh, Clay," she said, throwing her arms around his neck and burying her face in his shoulder. "Oh, I'm so glad it's you. I thought it might be one of those awful men."

Her lips sought his and they kissed for one long, happy moment. Then Shannon put his arm around her waist, took the reins of her horse, and led both of them up to the little cave.

Shannon now saw why he had mistaken Kathy for a man when she was riding toward him. She was dressed in boots, blue jeans, one of Shannon's flannel shirts, and an old winter coat. She was shivering, although whether it was from the cold or from fright he could not tell. He wrapped a blanket around her and sat down beside her.

"Kathy," he said, "what the devil are you doing here? I thought you were back in Whiskey Creek."

She leaned her head against his shoulder. He put his arm around her and felt the quivering of her body.

"I didn't want to stay there any longer," she said. "It was horrible. The house was so empty with Bobby gone and you so far away. I couldn't just sit around wondering if you were still alive or what dangers you might be facing. I had to try to find you. I just had to."

She bowed her head and took a deep breath, then looked up at Shannon. Her face was gray with strain and fatigue, but her voice was now steady.

"Besides," she said, "this isn't just *your* manhunt, Clay. It's mine, too. I want to help."

"But how did you find me?"

"I knew you and Pedro were going north out of Half Moon City. The marshal there told me about the cabin you were searching for. I decided that if you could find it, so could I, and perhaps you would still be there."

"But I wasn't there, so how did you know where to look for me?"

"I met Pedro coming down the mountain. He told me everything that had happened, about the gun battle at the cabin and the men you killed, and he explained that you had gone on after the rest of the gang. He told me you and he were planning to meet at the Indian agency in a few days, and I thought that if I didn't find you out here I could at least go to the agency and wait for you."

"Blast Rodriguez," Shannon grumbled. "He should never had let you come on alone."

Kathy sat up. Her voice now had a slight edge to it.

"He didn't *let* me come on," she said. "In fact, he did everything he could to try to persuade me to go with him, and even swore that if he had to he'd tie me to the saddle and take me back to Half Moon City that way."

"Then how did you . . ."

"I told him I wasn't going back and then I put my horse into a dead run up the hill. Pedro tried to follow me, but he had the other horse and the travois and the injured man. I knew he couldn't catch me, so I just kept going until I lost him. Don't blame him, Clay. He did his best to stop me. As I was riding away he was yelling at me like a madman, cursing in Spanish and calling for me to come back. He was as mad as a whole nest of hornets. He'll probably never speak to me again."

"But why did you do it, Kathy?" Shannon said irritably. "A woman in these mountains alone and traveling in the dark! You don't even have a blanket, much less any food or anything else that's needed for survival out here. And what if you hadn't found me? What if the outlaws had found you instead? Or another snowstorm had come up? Or . . ."

"I wanted to be with you," she said simply. "Don't you understand, Clay? I *had* to be with you. Our only child is dead, so it's just the two of us now. My home is where you are. And I want to help you catch those men."

Shannon stifled the reproach that came to his lips. He realized that it was not anger he felt, but fear—fear for the woman he loved. She had taken a terrible chance. Fortunately, it had worked out all right. The bad part was that now she had found him, it meant he would have to turn back with her in the the morning and get her down out of the mountains, back to civilization. He would lose days in his quest, days that might make finding the outlaws again impossible. But that could not be helped, now. The first priority was his wife's safety.

"You're going back tomorrow, Kathy," he said. "I'll take you back to Half Moon City and then start out again. I won't let you risk your life chasing these men. These are unscrupulous, brutal, evil people. They wouldn't hesitate to kill both of us if they got the chance. You said it yourself— it's just the two of us now. I don't want to lose you in a gunfight in some forgotten corner of this wilderness."

"I can help," she repeated stubbornly.

"No, you can't," Shannon said. "You'll slow me down. I'll be worrying about you when I should be thinking of other things. Tracking men is my business, Kathy. I'm a professional at it. You're not. Let me finish what I've started. I want the men who killed our son, and I mean to find them. Then I'll come back to you. I swear it."

He reached out to her, but she pulled away. This time when she spoke her voice was like cold steel.

"No," she said. "I'm not going back. I'm going with you. My little boy is dead, and those men killed him. I want to be there when you catch them. I want to see them die. I have that right, and I won't be cheated out of it. So don't try to send me back, because I won't go. No matter what happens, wherever this thing leads us, I'm going with you. I mean it, Clay. I'm going with you."

Shannon sat in the darkness, dumbfounded. This was a side of Kathy he had never encountered before. The warm, smiling wife he had known for so many years had disappeared. This hard, angry woman sitting beside was a stranger. He was about to continue his protests when he suddenly realized that what she said was true. She *did* have the right to come along. Justice or retribution or revenge or whatever it might be called, she had the right to be there when it was achieved, regardless of what the risks might be. And then something else struck him. He didn't *want* her to go back. The strain of the past few days, the loneliness, the worry of not knowing how she was coping. . . . No, he didn't want her to leave. Despite his distress over the dangers that lay behind and ahead, he wanted her to stay with him.

"Come to think of it," he said, trying to concede gracefully, "it's true you're a pretty good shot with that rifle you're carrying. And I'm getting a little tired of my own cooking. I suppose I could use an assistant. Especially one as pretty as you are."

Suddenly she was in his arms, and for a little while the pain and the fear and the loneliness were gone, replaced by joy and warmth and love, and above all a sense of companionship that was as great as any they had ever known.

# Chapter Eighteen

They set out at daybreak. Shannon took the lead, and Kathy followed with the pack horse.

"Don't lose him," he said to her as he handed her the pinto's lead line.

"Don't worry about that," Kathy said. "Just be sure you don't lose me."

The sun was warm and Shannon urged the buckskin on at a rapid pace. There was no hope of following the outlaws' tracks now, but he continually scanned the terrain ahead for any sign that might tell him that Drago and his men had passed this way. Once or twice he found some marks where a horseman had strayed briefly from the path, but the prints were old and indistinct and half-buried in the snow.

They had ridden for several hours when Kathy called to him.

"Look, Clay, back in the trees!" she said, the tension evident in her voice.

Shannon looked, and saw a small horse standing motionless in a small clearing a few yards from the trail. The horse had a blanket on its back but no saddle, and rawhide reins dangled beneath its neck. Just ahead, the tracks of the animal showed where it had left the trail and moved into the woods. The hoofprints indicated that the horse was unshod.

"Indian pony," he said quietly to Kathy. "Get into those trees and dismount. Don't rush, but don't waste any time. We may have some of Sitting Bull's friends waiting for us out there, and I don't want to play General Custer today." He had spoken lightly because he did not want Kathy to see the depth of his concern. They could be in great peril here. There had been no Indian trouble in that part of the country for years, but one never knew what might happen, and the two of them would stand little chance against a marauding band of hostiles.

In the shelter of the trees, Shannon drew the Winchester out of its saddle scabbard and slipped off the buckskin's back, handing Kathy the reins. Then he moved forward a few feet, studying the Indian pony as it pawed hopefully at the snow, foraging for the grass that was not there.

"Wait here," he said to Kathy. "I'm going to take a look. Keep your eyes peeled. If you spot any more of them, yell. Then ride like the wind back down the hill. I'll keep them busy while you get away."

In response, Kathy pulled the rifle from her saddle and dismounted, dropping the reins of her mare and the pack horse into the snow.

"I'm not going to leave you," she said. "I can shoot well enough if it comes to that. You said so yourself."

Shannon opened his mouth to protest, but then thought better of it. He had gained a great deal of wisdom over the years, and he knew well enough that it is a wise man indeed, particularly a wise married man, who knows when to keep his mouth shut. He smiled to himself at Kathy's un-yielding determination, prouder of her than at any other time of his life.

He went back to watching the pony. It seemed calm enough, and there was no indication of other horses in the vicinity.

"I'm going to take a look," he said. "Cover me."

He approached the horse slowly to avoid startling it. It tossed its head as he drew near, but did not bolt. Shannon caught up the dangling reins and examined the animal carefully. It was seemingly in good health, had no apparent injuries, and the saddle blanket was still in place. Then Shannon saw the bloodstains on the blanket and the series of crimson blotches leading away from the pony across the snow.

He signaled to Kathy to stay where she was, then began to move slowly over the icy crust, following the line of blood spots. The snow was churned up along their track, and it would have been obvious to a far less experienced hand than Shannon what had happened. Someone, presumably an Indian, had been hurt badly, had gotten off or fallen off the pony, and had then crawled away into the woods. But why? What was the cause?

The blood spots led up a slight rise and then disappeared abruptly over a low bluff. Shannon cautiously leaned over the edge, his rifle at the ready. At the bottom of the embankment a young Indian boy lay motionless, half buried in a snowdrift. A pool of blood had spread out beneath him, staining the snow bright red.

Shannon waved to Kathy to come on, then made his way down the face of the bluff and dropped to one knee beside the boy. About fifteen years old, Shannon decided. Bullet in the back, lots of blood, might have hit an artery or an organ. Alive, but unconscious. No sign of a weapon. Clearly someone had shot the boy, who had then crawled away in an effort to escape his assailant. He had then fallen over the cliff and down into the snowbank. Shannon lifted him gently out of the drift and started back up the hill.

After a brief scramble, balancing both his Winchester and the limp form in his arms, Shannon reached the top and laid the thin body down in the snow.

"He's still breathing," he said to Kathy, who came hurrying up. "Half frozen and missing a lot of blood. Get some blankets and cover him while I get a fire going. We'll have to thaw him out a little if we're going to save him. He's about done for."

They wrapped the still form in blankets and put him next to the fire. Shannon dragged some deadwood from the trees nearby and piled it on the blaze. The bigger the fire the greater the danger that someone would see it, but the wounded boy's limbs and torso were cold to the touch and Shannon knew that unless the his body temperature could be raised, death would inevitably follow. Kathy tended to him while Shannon went back to get their horses and collect the pony before it wandered away. Then he retraced his steps to the trail and cast around for any indication as to who had shot the young Indian, or why. At length Shannon discovered three empty shell casings half buried in the snow beside the track. Three shots, one hit. The assailant must have been a very bad marksman. Shannon inspected the spent shells. They were .44-40s, once a common caliber in that part of the country, but now less often seen. Probably from a rifle. He tucked them into his pocket for future reference. As to the identity of the rifleman who had fired the shells, there was no clue.

"Clay," Kathy called, "he's waking up."

Shannon knelt beside her. The boy was moving his arms and legs restlessly and whimpering words that Shannon could not understand. Then he opened his eyes and looked up at Shannon. Fear showed in his face.

"It's all right, son," Shannon said. "We won't hurt you. Do you understand English?"

The boy just stared at him.

"We're friends," Kathy said gently. "Do you speak our language?"

The boy looked at her, and some of the fear left his eyes.

"Yes," he said. "I go to mission school one year. I understand."

"Who are you?" said Shannon. "What's your name?"

"My name is Little Hawk," said the boy. "Why you shoot me?"

"We didn't shoot you, pardner," Shannon said. "We found you in that snowbank over there with a bullet already in you. Can you tell us what happened?"

"White men," said the boy. "White men shoot me."

"What white men?" Shannon said. "Do you know who they were?"

"Not know. Many of them. Big men, with cruel eyes."

"Where do you come from?" Kathy said. "Where do you live?"

"Live on reservation. There, in valley."

"The Wind River Indian Agency," Shannon said. "Has to be—no other reservation around here. Little Hawk, can you hear me? Which way did the white men go after they shot you?"

"He's passed out again," Kathy said. "He must have been in that snowbank a long time. Look at his feet—they're frozen. Oh, Clay, what will we do with him?"

"I guess we're stuck with another rescue mission," Shannon said resignedly. First the trapper, now this. He had another duty to perform, another life to save, another setback in his search. But there was one great consolation—the riders the boy described must surely have been Drago and his henchmen. He was still on their trail, and not far behind them. If he acted promptly he might yet overtake them.

But the boy's presence made quick movement impossible. He was seriously hurt, unconscious, and obviously could not ride his own horse. To tie him over the back of the pony with that wound in his body would surely be fatal. After a brief discussion, it was decided that Kathy would take him on her mare, sitting him in front of her on the saddle so she could hold him and prevent him from falling, while Shannon led both their pack horse and the pony.

"If he regains consciousness, ask how many men there were and which way they went," he said.

"I'll try," said Kathy. "I don't know if he'll be able to tell us anything more, though. Even if he wakes up again, with that wound he'll be delirious. How far is the agency?"

"Not certain," Shannon said. "There's supposed to be a fork in the track somewhere up ahead. I believe the agency is another four or five miles beyond that."

"We'll have to hurry if we're going to save him."

"Yes," said Shannon. "We'd better get moving."

About noon they came to the moment that Shannon had been both wishing for and dreading. The road forked as he had anticipated, one branch climbing on into the mountains, the other stretching down toward the valley below. He dismounted and prowled the ground for a good fifteen minutes, but found nothing to tell him which route the bandits might have taken. It would be a straight gamble now— left or right, up or down, one way or the other. At another time, Shannon's instincts and his understanding of the outlaw mentality would have sent him to the left, up the mountain and further into the high country. But circumstances had him in their grip. He was concerned for the safety of his wife, he had agreed to meet Rodriguez at the Indian agency, and now it was apparent that the life of the boy,

Little Hawk, depended on them getting him to the agency without delay.

Not reluctantly, because he saw clearly where his duty lay, but sorrowfully, because he knew it meant abandoning the chase, Shannon pointed to the right fork.

"Agency's down there," he said. "Can you hold the boy on your saddle for another few miles?"

"I'll hold him," Kathy said. Her tone left no doubt that she was determined to do just that. It occurred to Shannon that, having lost her own child, Kathy was now resolved to save someone else's.

They started down the path that led to the valley far below.

The way was steep, and soon they were below the snow line. The trees thinned out, and only an occasional patch of snow was to be seen. In one way Shannon was relieved to be off the mountain and out of the forest, yet as they descended his thoughts remained behind him on the mountainside, among the drifted snow and the tall, dark trees. The lure of that other branch of the trail filled his tired mind, tormenting him with the knowledge that each step the buckskin took was carrying him farther away from the murderers he was pursuing.

## Chapter Nineteen

The Wind River Indian Agency was located beside a snow-fed stream that ran through the valley into which they were descending. A dozen wooden buildings, some with tin roofs, were clustered near the little river. Some of the buildings appeared to be winter lodges inhabited by members of the tribe, but the entire area was surrounded by the more traditional teepees, apparently the living quarters of those who preferred their own heritage to the confining walls built by the white man. Each structure, whether lodge or teepee, had wisps of smoke drifting from the top of it, and a blue haze hung over the entire community.

The largest structure at the site was the Indian agency itself. A trading post occupied most of the building, but at one side was a little office with a faded sign on it that said AGENT. As Shannon and Kathy approached, men and women began to come out of the lodges and the teepees. There were children, too, all staring curiously at the strange procession that had arrived so suddenly amongst them.

Shannon reined up in front of the office and climbed down. The agent, a dark, lean man with keen eyes, came out of the office and hurried to the side of Kathy's horse to inspect her burden.

"Little Hawk!" he exclaimed. "He's been shot. Did you do it?"

"No," said Shannon, irritated by the question.

"What happened to him?" the agent said, feeling the boy's forehead anxiously.

"Don't know," Shannon said. "Found him just like that, in a snowdrift. Gunshot wound, frozen feet. Figured we'd better bring him here."

"I'm obliged to you," said the agent. "Very much obliged. My name's DeWitt. Forgive me for asking if you were to blame. I see now that it was a stupid question."

He spoke a few words that Shannon did not understand to a group of women who were standing close by, staring and commenting among themselves. They rushed forward, lifted the injured boy gently down from the mare, and carried him into one of the lodges.

"Come inside, please," DeWitt said to Shannon and Kathy. "Got a fire going in the stove and some coffee just getting hot. You folks must be chilled through. Don't worry, ma'am," he added, seeing Kathy's troubled glance toward the lodge where Little Hawk had been taken. "He'll be well looked after. Some of those women are better doctors than any you'll find in the towns in this territory."

The warmth of the office was a pleasant change for them after the unrelenting cold of the days and nights in the snow-clad mountains. Shannon and Kathy took off their heavy coats and sat around the hot stove, drinking the agent's coffee and recovering their strength.

Shannon related the entire story to DeWitt, from the events at Whiskey Creek to the moment of their arrival on the reservation. DeWitt listened intently, a concerned look

on his face. When Shannon had finished, the agent sat back
in his chair and rubbed his chin.

"Likely enough you're right," he said. "The men who
shot Little Hawk were probably the bunch you're chasing.
We haven't had much trouble like that around here lately.
It's unfortunate that such people are in the area again."

"But why would those men want to shoot Little Hawk?"
Kathy asked. DeWitt shrugged.

"Maybe because they thought he'd tell someone he'd
seen them," he said. "Or maybe just because he's an Indian.
Sounds like the people you're after would do something
like that just for sport."

"They probably would," Shannon said bitterly. "They
seem to specialize in hurting children." Then he frowned
as something DeWitt had said belatedly registered in his
mind.

"You said you haven't had much trouble like this
'lately.' What sort of trouble have you had before, and
when?"

"Oh, about four months ago one of our men disappeared
while he was hunting up there," DeWitt said. "John Lone
Bear. Fine man. We've missed him here, I can tell you."

"When you say 'hunting up there,' you mean in the
mountains we've just come through?"

"Yes. Same area where you found Little Hawk. The supplies sent from Fort Arthur—that's the army post over the
next range—don't always arrive on time, so the men here
sometimes have to hunt to feed their families. Lots of deer
and elk up there."

"You never discovered what happened to the missing
hunter?"

"Not for certain. His horse came back without him. We
searched, but there was no sign of Lone Bear. We assumed
he'd been killed, or so badly injured he couldn't make it

back, but we never learned for certain. Many things can happen to a man alone in the mountains."

Shannon excused himself, went out to his horse, and returned with the beaded deerskin bag he had taken from Catlett's saddlebags in Half Moon City.

"This look familiar?" Shannon said.

"I'm not sure," replied DeWitt. "The people here make so many things like this, that—"

"Did Lone Bear have a wife?"

"Oh, yes indeed. Wonderful woman. She—"

"Could you get someone to ask her to come in here?" Shannon said.

DeWitt hurried away to find the wife of the missing John Lone Bear. In a matter of minutes he was back with her in tow. Shannon handed the beaded bag to DeWitt.

"Please ask her if she recognizes this," he said. DeWitt held the bag out to the woman. As she took it, her eyes widened. She clutched it to her breast and said something in her native tongue. DeWitt looked perplexed.

"She says it belonged to Lone Bear," he said. "She says she made it for him about a year ago. Please, Mr. Shannon, how did you come by it?"

"I found it in the saddlebag of one of the outlaw gang after I arrested him in Half Moon City."

"Did he say where he had gotten it?" DeWitt asked.

"No," said Shannon. "I had to shoot him before I found out."

"Oh, dear," said DeWitt. "What do you think it means?"

"I think it means we've just found out why Mrs. Lone Bear is a widow. If Drago and his gang have a hideout up in the mountains, they've passed this way before. Little Hawk may not be the first Indian they've shot for 'sport.' "

DeWitt explained to Lone Bear's wife what Shannon had just related to him. She replied briefly, still clutching the deerskin bag.

"She wants to know if she may keep the bag," DeWitt said.

"Of course," said Shannon. "It's hers anyway. Please tell her how sorry I am about her man."

"And I," said Kathy, touching the woman's arm sympathetically. "I know what it's like to lose a loved one."

The woman started to leave, then stopped and asked another question.

"I told her you shot the outlaw who had the bag," DeWitt said. "She wants to know if he died after you shot him."

"Oh, yes," said Shannon. "He died. Somebody else shot him, too."

DeWitt translated this, and the woman uttered one sharp syllable.

"She says 'Good!' " said DcWitt, looking paincd. "Dcar me, our people usually aren't vengeful like that."

"Mr. DeWitt," said Shannon with a glance at Kathy, "I can promise you that almost anyone can become vengeful when someone they love is murdered."

As John Lone Bear's widow was leaving the office, one of the women who had taken Little Hawk away came in. She spoke with DeWitt briefly, then nodded gravely at Shannon and Kathy and left.

"That was Little Hawk's mother," said DeWitt. "She says the boy is very weak, and his feet are in bad shape, but it is believed he will survive. She says you saved his life," he added, "and she asked me to tell you she's very grateful."

"I'd like to talk with Little Hawk if I may," Shannon said. "I want to ask him more about the men who shot him. What they looked like, how many there were, which way they headed—that sort of thing."

"You're going after them?" DeWitt said. "They've probably gone up into one of the high valleys. In the old days, many outlaws and renegades hid up there. Some of them built houses like fortresses to discourage interference. It's been at least five years since a lawman went up there. I remember the last one well—a deputy U.S. marshal. He didn't come back, and no one wanted to go looking for him."

Shannon smiled wryly.

"Point taken, Mr. DeWitt, but I'd still like to talk with Little Hawk," he said.

The agent took him into the lodge where Little Hawk lay on a bed of animal furs. The women were bandaging him and trying to warm his frozen feet. He was conscious now, and he recognized Shannon. With DeWitt interpreting, Shannon asked his questions, and Little Hawk tried to answer. There had been at least six riders, he said. He heard them coming and rode his pony into the trees to avoid them, just as he avoided all white men. But they saw him and began to shoot at him with their revolvers, laughing. The man who wounded him was using a rifle. He was big and had a beard. After Little Hawk was hit and had fallen off his pony, the men with revolvers started to ride into the trees toward him, so he began to crawl through the snow to get away from them. Then he fell down the embankment into the snowdrift, and could go no further. He would never have escaped if they had come after him, but the big man with the beard shouted something at them, and they turned their horses and went back, heading on up the trail.

"That help you any?" said DeWitt.

"Yes," said Shannon. "The man who shot him fits the description of Drago, and now I know how many there are and which way they went. Since they didn't come here, they must have gone the other way, further up into the mountains, just as you said."

"Surely you can't hope to capture six men all by yourself," DeWitt said, frowning. "Why, there may be even more of them holed up wherever they're going."

"I wasn't really planning on capturing them," Shannon said darkly. "I had something else in mind."

"But your wife," said DeWitt, smiling politely at Kathy. "Surely she won't go with you on such a dangerous mission."

"Oh, yes I will," said Kathy. "I *am* going. All the way." She did not return the smile.

Shannon decided not to reopen the argument with Kathy at that particular moment, so he let the subject of her accompanying him pass for the time being.

"Mr. DeWitt," he said, "we need to stay with you for a day or so. I'm hoping to meet a friend of mine who is supposed to join up with me here. When he arrives, he and I will go after the men who shot Little Hawk."

"Of course, Mr. Shannon. You're more than welcome. My modest little house is just behind the trading post. It has a spare bedroom—I'm not married and so have no children to occupy it, you see. You and Mrs. Shannon should be very comfortable there."

They ate at the table in Mr. DeWitt's small kitchen, relishing the hot food.

"It's simple fare," said DeWitt proudly, "but our men are excellent hunters and our women are excellent cooks. I hope you enjoyed it."

"Very much," said Kathy. "Thank you."

"Now tell me," DeWitt said, "when do you expect this friend of yours to be here?"

"Probably tomorrow, possibly tonight," Shannon replied. "Marshal Rodriguez rides hard when he has work to do."

"I'll tell the men of the village to watch for him. There's a great deal of resentment over the shooting of Little Hawk and the news about Lone Bear. It wouldn't do to have your friend attacked as he approaches."

"Look, Mr. DeWitt," Shannon said, "I don't know this

country at all, and neither does Marshal Rodriguez. Can you make some kind of a map for us, something that would help us if we can't pick up the tracks of the outlaws?"

"I'd be glad to do that for you," DeWitt said heartily. "In the years since I came here as agent I've learned quite a bit about the area, and some of our men know all there is to know about it. I'll get them to help me draw a map for you showing the locations known to be used by white men in these mountains. I'll go and get started on it immediately. We'll have it ready by morning."

He rose and beamed in turn at each of them.

"I'm sure you both must be very tired," he said. He smiled again at Kathy. "You may sleep without fear tonight, Mrs. Shannon," he added, "for you and your husband are heroes to the people of this community because of what you did for Little Hawk, and because you wish to punish those that injured him."

Lying in Mr. DeWitt's spare bedroom, Shannon slept without fear but not without dreams. The haunting images kept coming back, as in his tortured mind he saw again and again that terrible day in Whiskey Creek. He also found himself reliving the fight at the burning cabin—fire, blood, men silhouetted against the flames as they died. But Shannon was not the only one suffering from nightmares. Several times during the night he was roused from his own bad dreams when Kathy cried out in her sleep or awakened suddenly, trembling. Each time he soothed her, reassuring her until she went to sleep again. Finally, toward morning, sheer exhaustion claimed both of them, and they slept peacefully until long past daybreak.

The sun was well above the horizon when Shannon was awakened by a stir of activity outside the agent's house. He arose from the bed, dressed hurriedly, and slipped out the door as quietly as possible to avoid waking Kathy. Out-

side, he saw at once what was causing the commotion—
Pedro Rodriguez was coming down the path toward the
agency. He waved nonchalantly to Shannon as he dismounted and tied his horse to the hitch rail outside the
trading post.

"So, amigo, I have at last caught up with you," he said.

"Well done," said Shannon. "How's McBride?"

"He is expected to recover. I delivered him to the doctor
in Half Moon City, who said that the McBrides of the world
are too ornery to die. But tell me quickly—is Señora Shannon with you? Is she safe? I have been most concerned."

"She's here. Thanks for trying to stop her from coming,
but I couldn't get her to go back either. I don't think anybody can. She's changed, Pete. There's a hardness in her
I've never seen before."

"She has suffered," Rodriguez said, "and she is angry.
Anyone would be under the same circumstances. Do not
worry, amigo. Underneath it all, she is still the same
woman you married."

"She wants vengeance," said Shannon. "She wants
*blood.*"

"So do you, my friend," Rodriguez said, looking keenly
at him. "So do you."

As Shannon and Kathy and Pedro were finishing their
breakfast, DeWitt came in, followed closely by a wiry Indian who regarded Shannon with a considering eye.

"How is Little Hawk this morning?" Kathy asked.

Dewitt looked sorrowfully at her.

"He will live, but his right foot could not be saved. It
was too badly frozen. They amputated it this morning."

"Oh, no," Kathy said. "That poor boy. What a terrible
thing to happen to someone so young."

"Indeed it is terrible, Mrs. Shannon," said DeWitt, "but

he is alive, and for that we must thank you and your husband."

He held up a folded piece of deerskin.

"Here's your map," said DeWitt. "I hope it will help."

"Thank you," said Shannon, taking it. "It's very kind of you to prepare it for us."

"We may be able to offer you something more than a map," said DeWitt, "if you're inclined to accept it. This is my friend Walking Elk. He's Little Hawk's father, and he wants to make a suggestion."

Shannon shook hands with Walking Elk and introduced him to Kathy and Pedro Rodriguez. Then, at DeWitt's invitation, they all sat together around the table.

"Mr. Shannon," said Walking Elk when they were seated, "I owe many thanks to you and Mrs. Shannon for what you did for Little Hawk. Had you not cared enough to aid him, he most surely would have died."

"It was nothing," Kathy Shannon said. "Anyone would have done the same."

"With respect, Mrs. Shannon," Walking Elk replied, "I fear that not everyone would have done anything of the kind. Not in this country. And not for an Indian. No, what you did was admirable, and I am deeply in your debt for it. Little Hawk's mother asks me to extend her deepest appreciation as well."

"You certainly speak English beautifully," said Kathy. "I wish I was as fluent in your language as you are in mine."

"Thank you for your courtesy," Walking Elk replied. "When I was younger I was fortunate enough to be sent by a charitable organization to a school in the East, and I tried to use the time wisely. But now I wish to speak of something else, something of greater urgency."

"Of course," said Shannon. "How can we help you?"

"It is I who wish to help you. As I said, I owe you a great debt, a debt of honor that according to the customs of my people must be repaid. Furthermore, and also according to the customs of my people, I wish to seek out the men who tried to kill my son. Because of their brutality, he is crippled for life. He cannot seek justice for himself, Mr. Shannon, so I must seek it for him."

"We're going after them," Shannon said, "Marshal Rodriguez and I. We'll find them, sooner or later, and on that day they will pay for my boy as well as yours."

"I have heard of your loss," said Walking Elk, "and share your grief. But what you propose to do will be very difficult, even for brave men such as yourself and Marshal Rodriguez, because you do not know this country. You need more than a map, Mr. Shannon. You need a guide. And I know these mountains as well as any man alive."

Shannon opened his mouth to refuse the offer, but Kathy was too quick for him.

"Thank you," she said. "We'll be very glad to have your help."

"Kathy," Shannon said, "I don't think . . ."

"To refuse such a generous offer would be an insult, Clay. Isn't that so, Walking Elk?"

"You are a wise and perceptive woman, Mrs. Shannon," said Walking Elk. "You understand our customs. But you speak of going yourself? Surely . . ."

"To try to stop me from going would be an insult to *me*," Kathy said. Her smile was suddenly a little frosty. "We have our customs, too. And you were more fortunate than we—at least your son is alive. Ours is dead, murdered by these very same men we speak of. I too desire justice, and I intend to be there when it is done."

"Is this your desire also, Mr. Shannon?" said Walking Elk. "To have Mrs. Shannon accompany us?"

"No, it's not," said Shannon, "but I think she's going with us whether I desire it or not." He said it with a laugh, trying to make light of the matter, but in truth he was becoming frustrated by his loss of control of the situation. He felt comfortable riding with Pedro Rodriguez, for Rodriguez, in addition to being an old friend, was a lawman like himself. But against his will, his wife insisted on placing herself in danger, and now this stranger was offering—or was it demanding?—to join the hunt as well. It seemed to Shannon that his private war was widening rapidly. He had always preferred to hunt wanted men alone, but now, despite his wishes, he had involuntarily collected what seemed to him to be a small army. Indeed, at this point it would not have surprised him if a troop of U.S. Cavalry had appeared, expecting to ride with him.

But then he realized that this was his pride talking, rather than his common sense. There were at least a six of the bandits left, and more might be waiting for Drago in the mountains. The simple fact was that, whether he liked it or not, he needed all the help he could get. Furthermore, the greater the size of his force the less danger there would be to Kathy. Therefore, he must accede to all this unwanted assistance.

*Until we find them*, he told himself. *I will accept help until we find them. Then Drago is mine, and mine alone.*

"Thank you for your offer, Walking Elk," he said. "I will be honored to ride with you."

## Chapter Twenty

They began saddling their horses, checking weapons, and preparing for departure. As Shannon was tightening the cinch on the buckskin, Walking Elk came over to him. There was a look of grim expectation on the Indian's face.

"I have spoken with several of our people," he said, "and we believe the men you are looking for may have gone to a certain valley high in the mountains northwest of here. It was once a place where white men attempted to graze their sheep in the summer. It was not a successful venture. The sheep have gone and the sheepmen have gone, but the house where the ranchers used to live while pasturing their animals is still there."

"Why do you think Drago's gang is holed up there?" Shannon asked.

"It is an ideal refuge for men wanted by the law," said Walking Elk. "It is isolated, strongly built, difficult to approach unseen. Bandits have used it before. Furthermore, about ten days ago two of our people were hunting near

153

the small valley where this place lies. They saw smoke coming from the chimney of the house, and some men riding away toward the south. There were also horses in the stable that stands nearby. It may not be the same men, but it seems to be a good possibility."

"How far is it from here?" said Shannon.

"The distance is not great. Twenty miles, no more. But it is very rough country, and during the last part of the journey we will be riding overland through some extremely harsh terrain. Still, I think it is our best chance."

"Good," said Shannon. "Let's go take a look."

"I have seen this place myself," Walking Elk said. "It is like one of the Yellow Stripes' forts, made of stone and easy to defend. If the men we seek are there, and they wish to fight, it will not be easy to overcome them."

"We'll worry about that when we get there," Shannon replied. "You say it's difficult to approach without being seen. How difficult? Can you bring us close without allowing anyone inside to see us coming?"

"Oh, yes," said Walking Elk. "That part will be simple. It will be what happens afterward that will be difficult."

He started to go to his horse, then paused and came back.

"There is one other thing you should know, Mr. Shannon," he said. "There is a another storm coming, a very big one. It may be the worst we have had in a long time."

"How soon will it arrive?" Shannon asked. He himself could see no signs of an approaching storm, but he knew that Walking Elk's people, living close to nature as they did, would have a weather sense that far exceeded his, an ability to anticipate weather changes long before the telltale signs were visible to his own eyes.

"It will come very soon," said Walking Elk. "We must be prepared for much wind and snow. We may have to shelter along the way if it becomes too bad. It is possible that we could be trapped in the mountains for days until the storm goes away."

"We'll have enough food to wait it out if that happens," Shannon said.

"Yes, we have enough for a week, possibly ten days. But it will be a bad time. Very bad. Your wife—she is a strong woman, but there will be a risk. Do you want to ask her if she wishes to continue?"

"I don't have to ask her," Shannon said, glancing over at Kathy as she was preparing to mount. "Nothing, not even the worst blizzard in history, is going to change her mind."

They rode single file, with Walking Elk in the lead. Shannon followed, with Kathy close behind and Rodriguez guarding the rear. Despite what he had said to Walking Elk about Kathy not changing her mind, Shannon had decided to try once again to persuade her to remain at the agency. He told her about the possibility of a storm and used that to try to discourage her from coming, but his prediction to Walking Elk was correct—she would not relent. Shannon was proud of her fearlessness but troubled by her intransigence. Always in the past when there was a difference of opinion between them about something, Kathy had been diplomatic, reasonable, willing to compromise. Now there was no compromise in her. It was as if on this one issue her will had turned to iron. Shannon could have forcibly stopped her from coming, but he feared that if he did so it would be an act for which she would never forgive him. So strongly did she feel that if he deprived her of the opportunity to be present when the men who had killed her child were found, he might lose her love forever, and that he did not want to do. And, in his heart, he knew that what she had said so vehemently before was still true—she had the right to come, whatever the risk.

So they rode together, with Shannon's mind filled with

misgivings about his wife's safety and perplexity about the change in her. Was Rodriguez right? After this was all over, would she still be the same woman, the woman he married, the woman he loved? He feared that she might not, and the thought disturbed him deeply.

But now they were well on their way, leaving the agency far behind them, and there was no more time for misgivings. Kathy had made her choice, and that was that. Now Shannon had a job to do, and he must concentrate on it to the exclusion of all else if any of them were to survive.

Soon they reached the fork in the trail where the day before Shannon and Kathy had abandoned the pursuit to take Little Hawk to the Wind River reservation. This time they took the other branch, following a rugged, uphill track that became ever more steep and rocky. Before long the trail dwindled to a narrow path, and the narrow path soon became a mere trace. After that, there was nothing—just the forest and the snow.

They climbed for more than two hours, the horses picking their way hesitantly over the rough ground that lay hidden beneath the drifts. Once Kathy's mount stumbled, and it occurred briefly to Shannon that the horse might have injured itself, thus forcing Kathy to go back, but the animal recovered its footing and plodded on, showing no signs of distress.

As they rode, the sky that had been bright and clear gradually became overcast, disappearing behind a dark, leaden blanket that blotted out the sun and transformed the day into an ominous twilight. Snowflakes began to fall, gently at first and then more heavily. Soon the wind increased, its keening note becoming more insistent by the minute. Before long the snow was driving into their faces, stinging their cheeks and causing them to hunch down in their saddles against its bite. Walking Elk had called the turn correctly—it was obvious that they were in for a major storm.

Without the sun to guide him, it was hard for Shannon to be certain of their direction, for he was following Walking Elk rather than depending upon his own navigation. However, he could detect from the changing direction of the wind that they were traveling in a wide semicircle, no longer climbing but moving slowly downhill so that the wind was now at their backs.

At length Walking Elk halted his horse, raising his hand to warn the others to do likewise. They waited as he dismounted and moved forward through the trees, disappearing from their view. The snow was starting to form new drifts, even in the trees, and as they waited it began to build up an icy crust on their coats. Sitting there motionless, they felt the cold more intensely. The horses moved nervously, unsettled by the gusting wind.

Then Walking Elk was back, standing at Shannon's stirrup.

"The house I spoke of is just ahead of us," he said, "and there are people there. We are very close, so we must go as silently as possible. The wind will cover the sound of our approach to some extent, but it is blowing from us toward the house and it would not do to be careless."

They left the horses and went forward on foot, following Walking Elk closely and trying to avoid stepping on the dead limbs that littered the ground beneath the snow. At last Walking Elk stopped, crouched down, and beckoned them to join him.

Shannon found himself on the edge of a rocky knoll. Below them, just visible through the falling snow, was a small ranch house sitting a hundred feet clear of the tree line, near one edge of a broad expanse of open ground. Presumably this field was a mountain meadow where sheep had once grazed in the warmer months of the year, but now it was just a featureless sheet of snow, with no cover to hide anyone approaching the house.

The building itself was made of stone, the individual rocks cleverly fitted together with some sort of mortar or mud plastered between them. It had a low roof which presumably was made of slate, but it was impossible to tell because it was covered with a foot or more of snow and ice. The windows of the house were heavily shuttered, and there were firing ports in the thick wood. Whoever had built the structure had done so with an eye to defending it if necessary. Whether the sheep ranchers had feared Indians or outlaws or something else in the days when they were constructing it could only be guessed at now, but clearly they had provided themselves with a solid place of safety in the event of trouble of any kind. A large barn or stable stood adjacent to the main house, capable, by Shannon's estimation, of holding a dozen horses quite easily.

Pedro Rodriguez was at Shannon's elbow.

"A formidable place," Rodriguez said. "It will be very hard to get at them behind those stone walls. The ground around it is completely open, and they would have a clear field of fire through the firing ports in those shutters. If they see us coming, they will surely cut us to pieces before we even get near the door."

"There is another concern," said Walking Elk. "We still don't know if these are the men we are after. It is likely, but by no means certain."

Shannon felt a moment of panic then. What if they had come to the wrong place? He could not begin arresting people, much less shooting them, until he was sure they were the ones he sought. But how to find out without risking the lives of his companions?

Kathy was just behind Shannon, watching over his shoulder.

"If it is Drago and his men, Clay, what will we do? How can we get at them?" she said.

Shannon did not reply. He was weighing the options.

"We might be able to starve them out," said Rodriguez, "but by that time we ourselves would be starving and also buried under ten feet of snow. It seems we have a challenging task ahead of us, amigo."

"Challenging," said Shannon, "but not impossible." He stole a quick look at Kathy. She was shivering.

Walking Elk had noticed her discomfort also.

"We must act soon, Mr. Shannon," said Walking Elk. "The weather is getting worse, and before long we will have to find shelter if we are to avoid freezing to death out here. Shall we retreat and come back after the storm is over?"

"No," said Shannon. "I'm not leaving until I know if these are the people we're after."

The front door of the house opened and a man came out. He was muffled in a long winter coat, and he bent over as he hurried from the main house to the barn. He opened the barn door and disappeared through it. Even against the wind Shannon could hear horses moving about inside.

"Did you recognize him, Clay?" Rodriguez asked.

"No," said Shannon. "I'll get a better look at his face when he comes out again."

They waited for what seemed an eternity.

"What is he doing in there?" Rodriguez grumbled. "He could have fed a hundred horses by now."

The man who had entered the barn came out and started to walk hastily across the intervening ground back to the main building. As he did so, he raised his head and looked fleetingly up into the storm. Shannon gasped, his eyes riveted on the upturned face. The man was Bully Drago.

"What is it, Mr. Shannon?" said Walking Elk. "Is it one of those you seek?"

"Not just one of them," Shannon said. "*The* one. The man who threw my son down into the street to die, and probably the same man who shot Little Hawk."

Drago had reached the house. The door slammed behind him, and once again there was no sound except the whining of the wind.

Kathy was beside Shannon now, holding his arm. There was a strange light in her eyes, and she was trembling, not with the cold but with excitement.

"Was it really him, Clay?" she whispered. "Was it really the same man?"

Shannon's breathing had become heavy, and his heart was racing. After all the days and all the miles and all the dangers, the prize he sought was now almost within his grasp. Elation flooded through him, the same elation he had felt during the fight at the log cabin. His fingers closed tightly around the cold metal of the Winchester in his hands. *Soon, now,* he thought. *Very soon.*

"Please, Clay, answer me!" Kathy said. "Is it him?" She was pulling at Shannon's coat sleeve to get his attention.

"It was him," Shannon said.

"Are you sure, my friend?" said Rodriguez. "We must be sure."

"I'm sure," Shannon said. "It was Drago, all right. And he's dead. He doesn't know it yet, but he's dead."

"You will not merely arrest him?" said Walking Elk. "You will kill him for me?"

Shannon hesitated, realizing the import of what he had just said about Drago being a dead man. A lifetime of playing by the rules, of enforcing the laws of his society, was colliding head-on with the burning hatred that was now consuming him. Only once before in his life had he broken the rules and put aside the law to make his own. Would he do it again now? Then it occurred to him that in reality there was nothing to decide. Drago would decide it for him.

"I'll try to arrest him," he said, "but he won't surrender. I'll have to kill him regardless."

"I wish I could kill him," said Walking Elk, "but it is your right. Yours and Mrs. Shannon's."

"Perhaps we should kill him twice," Rodriguez said with a bleak smile.

"Once will do," Shannon said, checking the cylinder of his six-gun. "Once will do quite nicely."

## Chapter Twenty-one

Shannon beckoned to the others and they moved back to where the horses were tied, out of earshot of the house. Animals and humans huddled together for protection against the storm.

"Are we going to rush them?" Rodriguez asked.

"No," Shannon said. "What you said a moment ago was exactly right. If they're keeping watch from those windows, long before we got to the door they'd see us coming and cut us down."

"Then how can we reach them?"

"You can't. I will."

They stared at him in dismay.

"Clay, you can't go out there alone," Kathy said. "It would be suicide."

"Yes," said Rodriguez. "If we all attack together, it will divide their fire and give us a better chance of reaching the house alive."

"And then what, Pete?" said Shannon. "There could be

ten or twelve men in there. Even if all four of us made it to the door, it would still be suicide. No, we've got to get them out of there, out in the open, and do it in such a way that we'll have the edge on them when they come out."

"I sense that you have a plan, my friend," said Rodriguez with a grin. "Share it with us, *por favor.*"

"It's very simple," said Shannon. "In a few minutes I'm going to get on my horse and ride out there as slowly and quietly as I can. They may be keeping watch through the shutters, but in a storm like this they aren't likely to be expecting company. Even if they have posted a lookout, one man approaching from the rear might escape detection. The odds are good I won't be seen, and with this wind they probably won't hear me either. When I get to the house, I'm going to invite them outside, and I think they'll accept the invitation."

"What do you wish us to do?" said Walking Elk.

"Get right up to the edge of the tree line where you've got a good view of the house," Shannon replied. "Keep your rifles ready. When they come out, they'll probably come out shooting. If so, cut down on them, and shoot straight. I don't know how many of them will be left by then, but don't take any chances with them."

"What do you mean by 'how many of them will be left?' " asked Rodriguez. "Left after what?"

"I'll show you," Shannon said.

He went to his horse, reached into one of the saddlebags, and took out the six sticks of dynamite he had purchased in Half Moon City. Kathy took in her breath sharply as she saw them.

*"Santa Maria,"* said Rodriguez. "Where did you get that, amigo?"

"Oh, back in Half Moon City," Shannon said carelessly. Secretly he was pleased with himself, for he had foreseen long ago that the outlaws would have a stronghold somewhere in the mountains, and that he might have to attack it. However, this was no time for self-congratulation. There was a dangerous task ahead.

"Pete," said Shannon, "how high would you say that roof is from the ground?"

"Five feet at the eaves, perhaps."

"And the peak of the roof?"

"Seven feet, no more. Very low."

"Yes," said Shannon. "Very low." The builders of any structure in the snow country would want low walls, because of the extra work involved in making them higher, and they would not want a high ceiling inside because that would waste heat, making it harder to keep the place warm.

"What about the chimney, Pete?" he went on. "Would you say that a man on horseback could reach the top of it?"

"A tall man, yes," said Rodriguez. Then his face lit up. "Ah," he said. "I see what you are going to do!"

"*What* is he going to do?" cried Kathy.

"I'm going to take some of this dynamite," Shannon said, "and drop it down the chimney. When it lands in the fireplace the men inside will see it or hear it, realize what it is, and come piling out of that door as fast as they can. They'll be so afraid of the dynamite that they won't stop to think about what may be outside waiting for them. But we'll be out here, and with luck we'll bag all of them at once."

"But surely," Rodriguez said, "some of them will still fight."

"Yes," said Shannon, his face blank. "Some of them will. But then, that's their choice, isn't it?"

"And some may be killed by the explosion," Kathy said. "That's what you meant about some of them being left, isn't it?"

Shannon nodded.

"There's always that chance," he said. "I don't know

much about what happens when you toss dynamite down a chimney into an open fire. If I cut the fuses too long the dynamite may merely burn, and all I'll have done is make their cozy hearth a little warmer. If I cut them too short, the dynamite may explode before everyone has gotten out. It might even explode before *anyone* gets out. Do any of you have a problem with that?"

"No," said Kathy. "Those men are killers. The fewer who come out, the less chance of one of us getting hurt."

"Precisely," Shannon said. "It's them or us. I prefer us."

"But," said Kathy, "if the dynamite goes off too soon, you could be caught in the explosion yourself."

"Yes," Shannon said with a shrug. "Anybody got any better ideas?"

No one spoke.

"All right, then," Shannon said. "Let's stop talking and go to work."

From his other saddlebag he produced blasting caps and a coil of fuse. Working carefully, he cut the fuse into short lengths and inserted each piece of fuse into a cap. Gingerly he crimped the detonators around the fuses and then slid one of the assemblies into the end of each of the six sticks of explosive. Next, he trimmed the inserted fuses down until they were very short, so short that they barely protruded beyond the detonator.

"How much of that are you going to use?" Rodriguez said, eyeing the dynamite.

"Let's try five sticks," Shannon said. "Since our lives may depend on this, I'd rather use too much than too little. We'll save the last one for the Fourth of July."

He took some heavy string from his pocket and tied five of the sticks of explosive into a bundle. He stuffed the bundle into one of the deep pockets of his heavy coat and slipped the remaining stick into the other. Then he mounted the buckskin.

"All set?" he said.

Kathy began to untie her horse.

"No, Kathy," Shannon said. "Not this time. I mean it. This belongs to me."

She started to object, but something in his voice stopped her.

"All right, Clay," she said reluctantly. "But be careful. Please, *please* be careful."

"Don't worry," Shannon said. "It'll work out fine." He leaned over and spoke to Rodriguez in a low voice so that Kathy would not hear. "Pete," he said, "if anything should happen to me, you and Walking Elk pull out fast and get Kathy back to the Wind River reservation. Forget about Drago and the rest of it—just get her to safety. Understood?"

Rodriguez hesitated, looking unhappy.

"I want your word, Pete," Shannon said sharply.

"Very well," Rodriguez said. "It shall be as you ask."

Shannon waved to them and started his horse down the hill.

He moved slowly through the trees, circling the house so that he could approach from the rear. Now on level ground, he paused in the edge of the woods to study the house. It remained quiet. Only the smoke from the chimney indicated that anyone was inside.

"Let's go, pal," Shannon said to the horse. "Death or glory."

Shannon rode out of the trees. He held the buckskin in a slow walk as he crossed the open space between the forest and the house. He almost stopped breathing, so intent was he on watching the building for any sign of movement. The seconds seemed like hours as he approached the house, sitting straight in the saddle, bracing mind and body for the impact of the first bullet. Seventy-five feet to go. Fifty. Twenty-five.

The bullet did not come. He reined the buckskin in close enough to the back wall of the house to reach out and touch it, then eased the horse sideways until its flank was almost against the snowy stones.

Shannon looked up at the chimney. This was the moment of truth. If he had judged the height of the roof and the chimney correctly, his plan should work. If he had not, well . . .

Shannon took a quick glance back at the hillside. Kathy and Rodriguez and Walking Elk were in position, crouching behind rocks and trees, just barely visible to him through the driving snow. He saw that, like the others, Kathy was holding her rifle firmly at the ready, preparing to give him covering fire.

*I'm a lucky man,* Shannon thought, *to have a woman like that.*

He slipped the tied bundle of dynamite out of his coat. Then, standing up in his stirrups and extending his arm as far as possible, he reached up toward the smoking chimney. His outstretched hand cleared the top by six inches. For a moment Shannon held the deadly package suspended there, bracing himself for whatever was going to happen next. Then he took a deep breath and shoved the dynamite hard down the chimney. He heard the bundle bounce against the sides of the flue as it fell, and there was a faint thump as it landed in the fireplace inside the house.

Immediately there came muffled cries of alarm, the crash of overturning furniture, and the sound of running feet. Shannon wheeled the buckskin and kicked it into full gallop away from the house, trying to reach the relative safety of the trees. Kathy's warning flashed through his mind—if the dynamite went off too soon, he might not get away in time.

The door of the house flew open and men began pouring out, wild-eyed with panic. Some of them were bootless and two were clad only in their red flannel underwear. The expression on their faces as they fled from the house was one of sheer terror.

Two of the men were still struggling to get through the doorway when the house exploded. The detonation blew pieces of the snow-covered roof a hundred feet in the air, and the stone walls came flying apart, sending shards of rock whipping past Shannon as he rode for cover. The effect of the blast hit Shannon in the back like a hammer, and his eardrums nearly burst with the sudden pressure. A piece of one of the disintegrating walls struck the buckskin in the rump. The surprised animal lost its footing and went over into the snow. Shannon pulled his feet free of the stirrups as the horse went down. He landed heavily in a snowdrift and rolled over, twisting his body so he could see what had happened to the cabin. His ears were still ringing from the blast.

The dynamite had done its work. Whether all five sticks had exploded or only one, the devastation was complete. The roof had completely disappeared, and only two of the walls of the house remained standing. They also were partly destroyed and were leaning drunkenly on the brink of collapse. Smoke and rock dust obscured Shannon's vision for a moment, and then he saw that several bodies were scattered in the snow around the cabin. At least two men were still inside, their corpses blackened by the explosion.

But many of the outlaws had survived, and as they regained their wits they began peering through the snowflakes, looking for their tormentors. Despite the curtain of white swirling between them, they immediately spotted Shannon lying on the icy ground scarcely thirty feet away. Those that had six-guns drew them, shouting curses as they aimed their weapons at him. Shannon clawed for his Colt, but with his holster pushed into the snow under his right thigh, he knew that it was hopeless—he could never clear leather in time. They had him.

At that moment the tree line erupted with rifle fire. Outlaws began to fall, cursing and shooting futilely at Shannon and at the trees even as they sank to the snow. Pieces of debris were still raining down on those who were left standing, and Shannon realized with a start that some of the debris was paper money. The bills must have been somewhere inside the house, and the explosion of the dynamite had scattered them. Now they were whirling merrily around the men who had stolen them, mixing with the snowflakes and then disappearing into the storm.

If the agitated outlaws were aware that their ill-gotten wealth was being blown away across the snow by the wind, they paid no heed. They began to run in all directions, still firing at Shannon and the rifle flashes in the edge of the trees. One man did not flee with the rest, but jumped up and ran directly at Shannon, cocking his revolver as he came. Shannon rose to his knees and fanned the hammer of the Colt. The man collapsed with a bullet hole in his throat. Another outlaw pointed his six-gun at Shannon, but before Shannon could react one of the riflemen in the woods behind him fired and the man went down.

Shannon looked around for more targets, but everyone he could see was already on the ground, killed or injured by flying rocks or Shannon's Colt or the fusillade from the trees.

Rodriguez and Kathy and Walking Elk came rushing out of the woods, still holding their rifles.

"No!" Shannon roared. "Kathy, get back!"

But Kathy never altered her stride. She raised her rifle and shot a man who was hiding behind the house's remaining wall, drawing a bead on Shannon's back.

"Clay!" she shouted, levering another cartridge into the chamber of the rifle. "Some of them ran into the stable!"

Shannon turned and raced around the remnants of the house, hoping to head off the surviving outlaws before they could get to their horses. As he came out of the shelter of the broken wall the wind howling down from the mountainside caught him full force, nearly knocking the breath out of him.

Wiping the stinging ice particles from his eyes, Shannon dashed toward the stable. Two of the gang had managed to mount their horses; they burst out of the stable door, nearly riding Shannon down. Shannon dived to the side and shot one of them out of the saddle as he went past. The last man hauled his horse around the corner of the stable and fled across the open field. Shannon cursed in frustration. The man who had gotten away was Bully Drago. Drago, the worst of them all, the monster who had killed his son, was slipping out of his grasp. Shannon emptied the Colt at him, but the distance was now too great for the six-gun and Drago rode on untouched, bending low over his saddle as he raced up the side of the mountain that towered above the little valley. His form faded away into the white curtains of snow.

Walking Elk was at Shannon's side.

"He gets away," the Indian said angrily.

"Oh, no," Shannon said. "That one won't get away. Not from me. Not now."

Shannon sprinted back around the house. Kathy and Rodriguez were bending over the fallen outlaws, checking to see if any of them were still alive. Shannon ran to his horse, praying that the animal was not seriously hurt. The buckskin was on its feet again, shaking itself to rid its coat of the clinging snow and apparently none the worse for wear. Holstering his empty six-gun, Shannon vaulted into the saddle and swung the horse around, urging him forward. In two strides the buckskin was at full gallop, flying across the snow after Drago's disappearing form.

"Clay! Clay!" It was Kathy's voice. "Clay, wait!"

But Shannon would not wait, not even for her. He yanked the Winchester out of its saddle scabbard and plunged on into the tempest, unheeding of his wife's frantic cries.

# Chapter Twenty-two

At the far edge of the open space the ground rose sharply upward. Shannon drove the horse up the steep incline, urging the animal to go faster. The buckskin responded valiantly, pitting its youth and strength against the slope and the storm. Once or twice, through the veil of blowing snow, Shannon could see the shadowy form of Drago and his black horse ahead of him on the mountainside. Shannon had to keep wiping his glove across his eyes to clear them of the icy flakes that continually formed on his eyebrows and eyelashes. The wind tore at him like a mad thing, but with his enemy in view, Shannon scarcely felt it.

On they climbed, Shannon and Drago, pursuer and pursued, until they passed out of the last of the trees onto a long, sweeping expanse of unbroken snow that swooped upward toward the top of the mountain, now lost from sight above them in the storm. Twice Drago looked back, and once he turned in his saddle to fire his rifle. The bullet must

171

have passed close to Shannon, but there was no way to tell, for the wind was drowning out all sounds except its own shriek.

The snow was deeper now, and both Drago's horse and Shannon's were laboring to make forward progress. The buckskin was sinking belly-deep into the drifts with each jump, its breathing as labored as its movement. Shannon saw that the chase could not continue much longer, because one or the other of the two horses would soon reach the limits of its endurance. He hated driving the buckskin so, for he loved the horse and would not have harmed it for the world. But his hate for Drago burned like a fire in his soul, and he wanted beyond all things to bring the outlaw to bay.

"Just a little more, old friend!" he cried to the horse. "Just a little farther and we'll have him!"

Then Drago's horse went down, floundering half buried in the snow. Drago pulled himself free of the fallen animal and fought his way through the white drifts to a cluster of ice-covered boulders. The horse struggled to its feet and went plunging away down the mountain. Drago swore foully at his departing mount and then swung his rifle over the top of the boulder and fired two more shots at Shannon. Both missed. Shannon leaped off the buckskin and ploughed his way to another clump of rocks just visible a few yards away.

And there they lay, facing each other.

Shannon remembered his oath, and his promise.

"Drago," he shouted, "you're under arrest! Put down the rifle and come out with your hands high!"

The wind brought Drago's laughter back to him.

"You're crazy if you think I'll let you take me, Shannon," the outlaw called. "You're going to die on this mountain, law dog! I'll leave you here full of lead and let your friends spend the rest of their lives trying to find your frozen carcass!"

Drago fired again, and this time the bullet knocked a chip off the boulder just beside Shannon's face. The rifle shot echoed up the mountainside, and a few clumps of snow came bouncing down the hill past Shannon.

Shannon was about to raise himself up to return fire at Drago when over the noise of the storm he heard someone thrashing up the incline behind him. He looked back to see who it was, fearful that another of the outlaws might be approaching, trapping him between two hostile guns. Then out of the storm Walking Elk appeared, rifle in hand. Shannon grabbed him and pulled him down behind the rocks.

"Look out, man," he said. "Drago will put a bullet in your brain if you give him a chance. How did you find me in this blizzard?"

"I tracked your horse," Walking Elk said. "You came a long way, Mr. Shannon. That buckskin of yours did well to climb so high. Many men have become lost on this peak and died here, buried beneath the snow. I thought that might be your fate too for a while, for the storm was so strong I could see nothing. Then I heard the shots and knew you had caught that devil Drago."

"Or he's caught us," Shannon said. He rested the Winchester against a rock and began reloading his six-gun. "Where are Kathy and Pete?" he said. "Are they all right?"

"They were not injured in the fight, but I do not know where they are. I jumped on my horse and followed you without waiting for them."

"Well, Drago's up there behind that cluster of three big boulders. He has a rifle and he's got a clear shot at us if we move. It's going to be tough to get at him, and I'm almost out of ammunition." He reholstered his revolver and picked up the Winchester again. "I'll try to bounce a bullet or two off those rocks," he said. "Maybe I can hit him, or at least get him to surrender when the ricochets start buzzing around his ears."

"To shoot any more up here would be dangerous," Walking Elk said, looking at the place where the dislodged snow had slid down past Shannon. "I know this mountain. It is a killer. Its face is steep and long, and the snow has been piling up here for several weeks now. A snowslide could occur at any moment. Even a single gunshot could bring the entire mountain down on us. It would kill us all."

"Maybe," said Shannon, "but I'll get Drago first."

He raised the Winchester to fire again at Drago, but Walking Elk put his hand out and pushed the barrel gently down.

"You have risked enough already," he said. "Now it is my turn." He had taken off his hat and was tying a beaded deerskin band around his head.

"I want Drago," Shannon said, his voice choking with emotion. "He killed my boy, and I want him."

"I will get him," Walking Elk said. "I will have vengeance for your son and for mine."

Before Shannon could stop him, Walking Elk had thrown down his rifle and drawn a knife from his belt. He rose, eluded Shannon's restraining hand, and darted up the steep, snow-covered hill directly toward the spot where Drago lay. As he ran he was chanting something in his own language, but whether it was a war cry or a hymn for the dead Shannon could not tell.

"Walking Elk!" Shannon cried. "Come back! You'll never make it!"

Drago was firing at Walking Elk now. With each shot little rivulets of snow came tumbling down the hill past them. As Drago fired his third shot, Walking Elk stumbled and clutched at his stomach, but then he resumed his headlong charge at the boulders where the outlaw lay. Shannon scrambled over top of the rocks in front of him and started after Walking Elk, still shouting for him to come back. Walking Elk sprang to the top of the low boulder behind which Drago was sheltering. The Indian raised his knife high, uttering one last terrible cry. Drago shot him in the chest. Walking Elk fell backward off the rock, landing spreadeagled in the snow. Drago jumped onto the rock, put his rifle to his shoulder, and fired point blank down at Walking Elk's prostrate form. Then Drago turned and ran on up the mountainside, disappearing into the veil of snow.

Shannon dropped down beside Walking Elk. The man was dead. Another of Drago's endless string of victims. Forgetful of his own safety, Shannon stood up and shook his fist at the blinding curtain of snow into which Drago had disappeared.

"Drago!" Shannon shouted. "You filthy coward, come down here and face me like a man!"

Drago's laugh came floating down to him out of the snow clouds on the hillside.

"Come and get me, Shannon," Drago shouted. "Come on up here and I'll give you just what I gave that sniveling little brat of yours. Did you hear him scream when I threw him down in the road, Shannon? Did you hear him scream?"

Maddened by Drago's taunt, Shannon raised his Winchester and fired again and again into the mist until the rifle's magazine was empty. As the hammer fell harmlessly on the vacant chamber, he tossed the rifle aside and drew his revolver. Colt in hand, he hurled himself up the mountain, fighting his way through the snowdrifts and the winddriven particles of ice. Suddenly the mantle of white parted and Drago was there, just a few yards ahead of him, crouched behind a rock outcropping. The outlaw was waiting for him, an unholy light in his eyes. Shannon threw himself down in the snow and scrambled into a small hollow that stood close by.

As soon as he was in it, he realized that it was too small to give him much protection. Drago, hidden behind much better cover, now held the upper hand.

Shannon rose up and fired at his adversary, but Drago merely ducked behind the rocks as the bullet went ricocheting off into space. Four more shots produced the same result.

Shannon was becoming desperate now. With his ammunition almost gone, he would have only a few more chances to bring Drago down. Once Shannon had fired his last cartridge, Drago could walk leisurely down and kill him at his pleasure.

Yet he could not hit Drago with the six-gun as long as the outlaw remained hidden behind his large outcropping. Something must be done to change the odds, and it must be done quickly. But what?

Then Shannon remembered the stick of dynamite in his coat pocket. He reached into the pocket and brought it out. The fuse and detonator were still in place. He fumbled in another pocket and found his small box of matches. The box was wet from the snow, and that meant the contents might be wet, too. Shannon hunched over and pulled one of the matches from the box. He scratched it on an exposed rock. Would it light? The match flared briefly and then was extinguished by the wind that was eddying around the boulders. Shannon opened the box again and extracted another match. He crouched down as low as possible to shield it with his body. This time the match burst into life. Swiftly, before the wind could blow it out, Shannon jammed the flame against the short piece of fuse in the dynamite. The fuse began to sputter, its sparks fanned by the persistent gale.

*I'll have to get the dynamite just beyond those boulders where Drago's hiding,* Shannon told himself. *If it falls short, the rocks will protect him. If I throw it too far, the blast won't have any effect on him.*

Knowing that he had only seconds to act, Shannon jumped up and hurled the dynamite as far as he could up the mountainside. It sailed over the rocks where Drago was hiding and landed in the snow several yards behind him. Hardly had it disappeared through the icy crust when it exploded, sending a geyser of dirty snow spurting high into the air. The blast was deafening, and the shock waves reverberated off the snow-covered heights of the mountain hanging above them, the echoes magnifying the sound a hundredfold.

Shannon did not care about the noise; his only concern was the explosion's effect on Drago. *Too far behind him,* Shannon thought as he dropped back into the shelter of the hollow. *I threw the dynamite too far behind him. The last stick, and I've wasted it.*

But it was not wasted. Drago, keeping his head down to avoid making himself a target for a bullet, had not seen Shannon throw the dynamite. Although the outlaw was not injured by the explosion, he was so startled by it that he jumped up from behind his rock and turned around to see what had happened. Instantly Shannon sprang up, thumbing back the hammer of the Colt. Drago, belatedly realizing that in his moment of surprise he had exposed himself to Shannon's gun, whirled back toward Shannon and raised his rifle. Both men fired at the same instant. Drago's slug tore into the flesh of Shannon's side, knocking the breath out of him. Yet even as he fell, Shannon saw that his own bullet had struck Drago low in the abdomen, driving him backward into the snow.

"Don't shoot! I give up!" Drago wailed, clutching his stomach. "I'm gut-shot! Help me!"

Shannon was in too much pain from his wound to feel any sense of triumph. He struggled to his feet and started up toward Drago. Then, after he had taken only a few steps, he stopped again. Something was wrong. From far above him there came a sudden rumbling sound, at first faint, then rapidly growing louder and louder. As Shannon listened, it seemed to him that the noise was approaching like some invisible express train hurtling down a long and deadly track.

*Avalanche,* thought Shannon. *The dynamite must have started it. Walking Elk was right—this mountain has killed us all.*

Shannon holstered the Colt and stood there, motionless, knowing that it was useless to flee. He could not outrun the avalanche, and in any event the thickness of the falling snow made it impossible for him to tell in which direction safety lay. And so he waited, listening to the escalating roar. Out of the grayness of the storm, his fate suddenly burst upon him—a huge wall of snow and ice traveling at incredible speed down the mountainside, coming straight at him. The great mountain shook beneath Shannon's feet as the thunder of the oncoming wall of death filled the air.

Shannon knew he should be afraid, but was surprised to find that he was not. All he felt was a profound sadness that his life was ending now, when he had so much to live for.

*Good-bye, Kathy,* he whispered. *A least I kept my promise. I got him.*

Drago was shrieking hysterically, struggling to rise as the avalanche rushed down upon him. Then the solid wall of snow struck him, swallowing him up, stifling his last terrified scream.

Shannon stood unflinching as the snow slide crashed into him. He felt the breath driven from his body as he was caught up in the icy flood and catapulted head over heels down the mountain. Something struck him on the head and he lost consciousness.

## Chapter Twenty-three

Slowly, painfully, Shannon opened his eyes. He was lying atop a jumbled heap of dirty snow that was piled high against a rocky ledge. He tried to move and then gasped in pain as he realized his leg was broken. Ribs, too, he told himself vaguely, still trying to regain his command of his senses. He felt blood dripping down his face, and put his hand to his head. Something had gashed his scalp badly.

He lay back for a moment, gathering his strength. It was obvious what had happened—the avalanche had carried him down the mountainside until it had at last expended its force against the rocks and the great trees that lay around him, ripped out by the roots and splintered like kindling. Somehow he had been carried along on the surface of the torrent instead of being entombed by it. And somehow, miraculously, he had survived.

Wincing with the pain, Shannon pulled himself up on one elbow and looked around. The wind had died away, but the snow was still coming down unabated. Through the murk, Shannon could see a body lying a few yards away from him, half-buried in the snow. The corpse's face was bruised and battered, but Shannon recognized the distorted features of Augustus "Bully" Drago, former outlaw and erstwhile murderer of children.

*I wish I could crawl over to you so I could spit on you,* Shannon thought. *But I suppose it makes no difference now, because now you feel nothing and you are nothing.*

He lay back again, dizzy and gasping for breath. His right side was torn where Drago's bullet had passed through it, and from the knifing pain that accompanied each breath he knew that the snowslide had broken at least one rib on the other side, probably several. He attempted to crawl down the slope, but the agony of his shattered leg overwhelmed him, and he lay there for several minutes, trying to keep from fainting. Finally he propped himself up again and looked down at the leg. His boot was twisted at an odd angle, and there was blood on the snow. *Compound fracture,* he said to himself. *Won't be traveling far with that.*

He had lost his hat, and the snowflakes were caking up in his hair and on his shoulders. He wiped it out of his eyes and looked around again. Now that the wind had stopped, the mountainside was uncannily quiet. It was also suddenly very lonely.

Then he heard a crunching sound on the hill above him. Out of habit he fumbled for the Colt revolver, and was amazed to find it still in its holster. It had been kept there throughout his pummeling in the avalanche by the rawhide thong which, out of long habit, he had unthinkingly slipped over the hammer before the cascade of snow struck him. He flipped off the thong and drew the six-gun, craning his neck to find the source of the noises he was hearing. The shroud of snowflakes parted for a moment, and he found himself looking at the buckskin as it plodded down toward him, picking its way carefully over the uneven footing. Either the horse had been far enough to the side to escape the hurtling wall of snow, or some freak diversion or forking of the avalanche had spared the animal. Whatever the cause of the buckskin's survival, Shannon was never so happy to see a horse in his life. The colt approached, then stopped beside him and gently prodded him with its soft nose. Despite the pain it caused him, Shannon could not help but laugh. At least this buckskin horse had not died because of his owner's foolishness.

Now the question was whether or not he could get into the saddle. Although the wind had gone, the cold was still piercing, and he had been lying in the snow, bleeding, for some time. If he did not somehow make it the rest of the way back down the mountain, his providential survival of the avalanche would be of little value, for he would freeze to death where he lay. He reached out to grasp the buckskin's reins, but as he did so his involuntary exclamation of pain startled the horse. It moved away a few feet and stood there, watching him with patient curiosity. He called out to the animal, but it only bobbed its head in reply, and when Shannon again tried to drag himself toward the horse it whinnied once, then turned and wandered slowly away down the incline and into the trees until it was lost from sight in the snow.

Shannon watched the buckskin's departure in consternation. Unable to walk or even crawl, his horse beyond his reach, his only chance now was that somebody would find him. Kathy and Rodriguez must be out there somewhere, looking for him. But how could they or anyone else locate him in this shroud of white that surrounded him, hiding him from view? In the welter of snowflakes, the searchers could pass a few yards from him and never see him. And even if they did see him, by then it might be too late. The cold was beginning to penetrate deep into Shannon's body, dulling his senses. He was getting drowsy, and drowsiness was, he knew, the first sign of freezing. Soon it would overwhelm him.

He must signal for help. Yes, that was the thing to do. He should have thought of it sooner! Three shots, spaced a few seconds apart—the universal signal of distress. Then another three and another three every few minutes until somebody found him. There was some danger of starting another avalanche, but at this point he had little to lose. Yes, he would fire shots until someone came.

He again drew his revolver and opened the loading gate to check the cylinder. He had one shell left. But there were more in his cartridge belt, surely. He could not have used all of his ammunition during the fighting. Ignoring the pain, he reached around, feeling for the belt loops with his numbed fingers. He had two cartridges left in the gunbelt. Only two.

*Well*, he told himself, *one and two make three. Maybe someone will hear. But even if they hear, can anyone find me in this weather by trying to follow the sound of just three shots?*

He withdrew the two remaining cartridges from the belt and slipped them into the cylinder of the six-gun. Then he held the weapon in his hand for a few moments, gazing down at it. The Colt had been with him through many adventures and saved his life many times. The ivory handles were yellowed now, and the midnight blue finish was beginning to wear in spots, but the six-gun had been his constant companion through the years, and it had served him well. Would this be the last time he ever fired it?

He pointed the gun at the sky, then cocked the hammer and pulled the trigger three times, very slowly. The reports echoed off the slopes, passing again and again along the face of the mountain. To anyone listening, the shots would seem to have come from a dozen different directions. It was hopeless.

Carefully he holstered the revolver and lay back in the snow. The drowsiness was becoming irresistible. As he drifted into unconsciousness, it occurred to him that he was no longer cold. Somehow the frigid air and the icy snow had become warm and comforting. It was a wonderful sensation. The pain from his injuries was gone, too. Perhaps freezing to death wasn't so bad after all. He looked over one more time at the body of the late Augustus Drago. The staring eyes seemed to be mocking him, saying "You see, I killed you, too. I told you you'd die on this mountain. Now you will." *But of course it's only my imagination*, Shannon thought as he drifted off. *Drago no longer exists. He's just yesterday's nightmare, a slab of cold meat rotting in a pile of dirty snow. I've won after all, Drago. I've won after all.*

As Shannon slipped away into unconsciousness, he began to dream. He saw again that last happy evening in the little house in Whiskey Creek, the delicious food warm upon the table and his wife and child beside him, laughing. He heard Kathy singing in the kitchen of her little café the night he had first met her, the blue dress starched and fresh upon her and her golden hair shining in the lamplight. He saw them walking together beside the river under the cottonwood trees, falling in love. He remembered the wedding at Whiskey Creek's new church, with Kathy radiant in her wedding dress and every soul in town turned out to wish them well. The birth of their son. The years of happiness together. The love he had shared with her. He could even hear her crying out his name. From somewhere, faintly, distantly, she was calling to him, but he could no longer see her.

*Good-bye, Kathy*, he whispered to her. *Good-bye. I have*

*to go now. I'm sorry.* Then he began the long slide into eternity.

But something was wrong. Kathy was still calling him. Her voice was moving closer, becoming more urgent. What did she want? Why was she trying to pull him back from his warm and beautiful dreams? He did not want to return. He just wanted to rest in the cozy darkness.

Then her voice was close beside him, loud and insistent.

"Clay!" she called. "Clay, where are you?"

He struggled back from the depths into which he was sinking. Suddenly it was cold again, and he could feel the snowflakes on his face. He was still alive, and it really was Kathy calling for him. With one final effort, he managed a single reply.

"Kathy!" he croaked. "Over here!"

And then Kathy was beside him and Pedro Rodriguez was beside him and Kathy was holding him in her arms, crying for joy.

"Oh, Clay," she said. "You're alive! You're alive!"

After that he became dimly aware that Rodriguez was tying a splint onto his broken leg, and wrapping some sort of bandage around his aching ribs.

"Easy, amigo," Rodriguez said. "It's a long way down this mountain, but we'll get you there. Come on, *hombres*, give us a hand."

Shannon found himself surrounded by horses' hooves, and several men—Mr. DeWitt and others whom he recognized from the Wind River Indian reservation—were lifting him gently onto a travois, throwing blankets on him, speaking to him in unintelligible but friendly tones.

"Where did all these people come from?" Shannon said, raising his head to look around.

"They followed us from the agency," Kathy said. "They wanted to help, too. Now lie back and rest—we'll take good care of you."

Shannon just had time to notice that the snow had stopped before the travois began to move, carrying him down from the dreadful mountain, down into the welcoming valley, down into the world that he had almost left. Kathy walked beside the travois, holding his hand.

Shannon's voice was hoarse, but he forced out the words.

"Drago's dead," he said. "I kept my promise."

"I saw the body," Kathy said. "He's finally paid for all the terrible things he did."

"Walking Elk is dead, too," Shannon said.

"We thought as much," Kathy replied. "The men from the reservation looked for him but couldn't find him. I imagine he was buried under the snowslide."

"Yes, I suppose so," said Shannon. "He was a good man, and he died very bravely."

"We won't forget him," Kathy said.

"What about the money Drago's men took from Whiskey Creek?" he said anxiously. "Did you find any of it?"

"Only a few bills. The wind spread the others all over the mountain."

"The bank's going to be unhappy with me," Shannon muttered. "They wanted it back."

"They'll forgive you," Kathy said. "You wiped out the gang—they ought to be very pleased by that. Besides, your life is more important than the money."

"Probably not to those bankers," Shannon said, "but it certainly is to me."

"Me, too," Kathy whispered.

Another thought struck Shannon.

"My horse," he said urgently. "The buckskin. He's out here somewhere."

"We found him. He led us to you."

"Always said that was a smart horse," Shannon mumbled. He was getting drowsy again, but this time it was not the approach of death, but the simple, healing sleep that comes to those who have worked hard, done their jobs well, and are closing their eyes for a few hours of well-deserved rest.

Then one last conscious thought occurred to him.

"Kathy . . ."

"Yes, Clay?"

"What I said before all this started—about quitting, about taking off the star. I've changed my mind. I'd like to keep it on. Could you stand being a lawman's wife a little longer?"

Kathy squeezed his hand. Shannon could see that tears of happiness were coursing down her cheeks. She bent over him and kissed him.

"Come on, Sheriff," she said softly. "Let's go home."